The Joker

By Debor⸺

Cover de⸺

North East England born Deborah knew from an early age that she wanted to be a writer. Life had other plans and for a while, writing was put on the backburner. Although it became a distant memory, the dream was never forgotten and she knew that her desire to write would one day push its way to the top priority.

Deborah now uses her life experiences and opinions to write posts for her own blog as well as guest posts for others. Her childhood dream did not stop at non-fiction she also had dreams of exploring her creative side by writing fiction. She welcomes you to her debut book!

To become acquainted with her work and for updates of new publications, visit www.myrandommusings.co.uk and you can also catch up with her on Twitter www.twitter.com/randommusings29

Prologue: Ireland 1973

Closing his bible, Father O'Malley takes several deep breaths. In. Out. In. Out. It calms him and he reaches for his handkerchief and wipes the sweat from his face, blinking rapidly as it stings his eyes.

He surveys the room. The child, sweet in her innocence looks back at him, wide eyed with terror, her pale skin emphasised by the candlelight in the dark room. Beads of sweat stand out on her face.

He turns to where her terrified parents stand clutching each other in the corner of the room.

His movement seems to break the spell that has gripped them, and the child's mother breaks from her husband's embrace, and throws herself towards the bed, clutching the child and holding her close, kissing her face, her head, breathing in her scent. Tears stream down her face.

'Is it her?' asks her husband, moving towards them.

'Yes,' replies his wife, never leaving go of her daughter. 'It's her, she's back. My little Rose is back'

Rose seems to respond to the voices of her parents, and begins to cry herself. Not the sobs of a young child, but the silent tears of a grown up, one who has seen too much and doesn't know what to do, what to think.

She pulls her head from her mother's breast, and looks around the room, her room, as if seeing it for the first time.

Her eyes settle on Father O'Malley.

'Thank you Father,' she says, her voice a mere whisper. Father O'Malley has to strain to hear her.

'You are welcome my child,' he responds warmly. 'You are safe now.'

Rose is comforted by his words, and the tears start to slow down a little. At twelve years old, Father O'Malley hopes that this incident doesn't affect her upcoming teenage years too much.

He turns to her father, as he stands beside the bed. 'The Demon is gone. He will not return. He has been banished back to the depths of Hell from where he emerged.'

'I don't know what to say Father, how can we ever repay you. I don't...'

Father O'Malley holds up a hand, silencing Rose's father. 'Repayment is not necessary, Mr Callahan. Simply remember to thank the Lord.'

Not waiting for an answer, the priest turns and leaves. His work here is done. Now he must return home and sleep. These exorcisms always take it out of him, and at 29, although he is not an old man, he feels older than his years after this experience. But he can rest easy, knowing the child is fine, rid of the evil spirit which took up residence inside her.

Maybe not entirely easy. Something about this exorcism niggles at Father O'Malley's mind. Something he can't quite place. He has been carrying out exorcisms for the last four years. He has encountered a fair few demons, this one in particular has put in several appearances over the years, and has always put up a strong fight.

The last time, Father O'Malley began to doubt if he could complete the exorcism alone. The demon was just too powerful. But this time, it was almost too easy. There had been very little fight left in the demon. The priest knew he should be pleased. The power of Christ was getting stronger, and the demon was getting weaker.

That didn't exactly ring true to him though. The demon didn't feel weak, if anything, he felt stronger than ever. It was as though he had left willingly, and this new turn of events was the thing that troubled Father O'Malley.

He pushed the thoughts to the back of his mind. After all this was, to all extents and purposes, a successful exorcism. He tried, unsuccessfully, to convince himself that his sense of foreboding was wrong. It was simple paranoia. He knew it was more than that, but it wasn't his problem now.

He knew he could never explain it to the bishop. He couldn't find the words to explain it, and even if he could, the bishop would simply tell him the demon was gone, and to let it go, the damage had been undone.

'When will people stop messing around with the spirit world, and unwittingly inviting these demons into their lives,' he ponders sadly as he reaches his door, shaking his head slightly.

As he reaches out to turn the door handle, he feels a sharp pain in his chest. He pulls his hand back and clutches the area. Another sharp pain. Another. He sinks to his knees, fighting for breath.

His hand reaches out, clawing at the door. His vision begins to blacken around the edges, and he lets out a moan with the little bit of air he manages to snatch.

The door bursts open and Mrs O'Keefe, his housekeeper is standing there.

'Father!' she exclaims, bending to help him to his feet.

'I…I…' he stammers, helplessly. He has to tell her what he was thinking. It doesn't matter if they think him senile. It is his responsibility to his church, his God.

'Don't try to talk Father,' she says. 'I will go for help.'

He knows it is too late, his mouth won't form the words. It opens and closes like a fish out of water. He tries to reach up, but he can't move.

He feels one final pain in his chest, the worst yet, and his vision goes fully black. He falls from his knees, landing on his side. His final earthly resting place.

Mrs O'Keefe stands back up, crossing herself, as tears start to run down her face.

Chapter 1

I take a sip from the whiskey bottle as Zach passes it to me. I feel the fire spread to my stomach, and pass it on quickly, my fingers brushing Kev's as he takes it from me, and the fire in my stomach is suddenly there for a different reason.

I feel like everyone in the room can feel the electricity pass between us and I squirm a little.

The tension is broken when Emma, my best friend, announces loudly 'I'm gonna be sick if I drink anymore of that stuff. What made you get whiskey off all things?'

I shrug. 'It was on offer.'

'I'm not surprised,' she slurs laughing.

We are about half way through our second bottle between the four of us, and we are all a little worse for wear.

I sit on the couch, sandwiched between my boyfriend, my official boyfriend, who I have had a thing for since forever, Kev, and his best mate Zach. Emma is sitting cross legged on the floor in front of us.

We are at Zach's place, as his parents are out for the night.

'Wanna play truth or dare?' asks Emma, a mischievous sparkle in her eye.

'We aren't twelve anymore,' retorts Zach.

For a second, Emma looks hurt, but she recovers quickly. 'Just a thought.'

'If you want to play a game, I've got the perfect one,' says Zach. 'Hold on.'

He leaves the room. Kev gets up and changes the music. I watch him as he looks at the CDs. Wow he is hot! Emma catches me checking him out and grins.

She opens her mouth to speak, no doubt something that would have embarrassed the life out of me, as Zach walks back in carrying a box.

'Here we go,' he says, putting the box down on the dining table at the end of the room.

'Don't be shy,' he adds, looking at us expectantly.

Kev walks over, offers me his hand and pulls me off the couch. I stumble slightly, and he catches me. The whiskey is doing the trick, that's for sure. We walk over to the table, where Zach has opened the box and pulled out a board.

'A board game? Lame,' says Emma, not bothering to stand up from her place on the floor.

'Not just any board game,' Zach counters, unfolding the board, and reaching back into the box.

From where I'm standing, I see its a Ouija board. His hand comes back out of the box holding up the planchette for Emma to see.

'No. Uh uh. No way,' she says the casual contempt on her face replaced with a frown. 'You shouldn't mess with the dead.'

'It's only a game. You chicken?' asks Zach, laughing.

That does it. Emma won't have him or anyone else thinking she is chicken. She walks over to the tables, pulls out one of the chairs and sits down. 'It won't work anyway.' She announces, the horror replaced with cockiness.

'One way to find out,' replies Zach sitting next to her.

'Come on guys,' he says to me and Kev, nodding towards the remaining two empty chairs.

I glance at Kev, and he shrugs and walks around the table, sitting down. I sit in the remaining chair, across from Emma.

'So how does it work?' asks Kev. I find it reassuring that his voice is normal, level, no trace of nerves or anxiety. Nothing bad will happen to me when he is here, I just know it.

Zach looks around at us, his expectant audience. 'We call up a demon and get him to carry out our evil deeds!'

Kev raises an eyebrow. Emma swallows audibly.

Zach laughs. 'I'm kidding! We put our fingers on the planchette and ask questions, and the spirit world will try to answer them. That's it.'

'So it's not dangerous?' asks Emma, her voice quiet, unsure. It's obvious to me she isn't into doing this, but she won't have Zach thinking she is scared. Oblivious, Zach carries on.

'Nope,' he responds. 'Totally harmless. Everyone put your fingers on,'

We do.

'A few rules,' says Zach. 'Do not, under any circumstances remove your finger from the planchette until I tell you it's ok. Be respectful, no joking around.'

I've never known Zach be this serious. 'So it is dangerous then?' I ask

Zach turns to me 'No more dangerous than crossing a road. You follow the rules, you won't get hurt, it's that simple.'

'Unless the driver coming up is a loony,' mutters Emma.

Zach ignores her comment. 'Let's begin. Everyone close your eyes. Don't open them until you feel the planchette start to move.'

I close my eyes.

Zach's voice makes me jump a little and I supress a giggle.

'Is there anyone who wishes to make contact with us?'

Nothing. I can't resist peeking. Opening one eye, I glance around. Emma, head down, looks a little pale. This really isn't her thing. I glance towards Kev; he isn't even being subtle – both his eyes are wide open. He catches me looking at him and rolls his eyes. I can't keep the giggles in anymore and snort out a laugh. Zach's eyes fly open.

'Be serious, or it's off,' he demands.

'Sorry,' I say, a little taken aback. Zach isn't known for being serious. Maybe this thing is more dangerous than I thought.

He continues to glare at me and I close my eyes fully this time, glad to break his gaze.

He tries again. 'Is there anyone who wishes to make contact with us?'

I swear I feel the planchette jerk slightly.

'Use our energy to give you power,' continues Zach.

I hear a low humming noise, like a fridge running, and the planchette moves for real this time, flying across the board. I open my eyes. The planchette is at yes.

I'm not convinced it's not Zach or Kev moving it, trying to give us a scare. I look at them one at a time, but neither of them are giving anything away in their expressions.

'What is your name?' asks Zach.

The planchette flies around the board. There is no hesitation this time, and it pauses only long enough to allow us to read the letters it points to. S-C-U-R-R-A. Scurra.

The planchette stops, waiting for our next question.

'Do you have a message for us?'

Yes, E-M-M-A, it spells out.

Emma jumps up, her chair flying backwards. 'You did that, you pushed it,' she yells accusingly at Zach, her breath coming a series of short, ragged pants.

Before he can answer, the lights dim and come back up again. The whiskey bottle, sitting forgotten on the table shatters. Emma screams. I want to scream myself but it's like I'm frozen. I sit with my finger still on the planchette, not daring to move, to speak.

Zach's voice is low and calm. 'Sit back down and put your finger back on. You have broken the circle and the spirit is angry.'

'Yeah, right,' Emma has regained some composure. 'You set this up, didn't you? Just admit it.'

'No,' replies Zach, still eerily calm. 'But if you really think that, you shouldn't be scared about putting your finger back on.'

Her bluff called, Emma turns around and rights the up turned chair. She sits, and puts her finger back on the planchette.

Zach turns his focus back to Scurra. 'What is your message for Emma?'

F-L-Y-L-I-K-E-A-B-I-R-D

I let out a breath I didn't realise I was holding. I'm surprised to hear Emma speak.

'What does that mean?' she asks in a quiet voice.

'I…' starts Zach.

'I'm not asking you,' she interrupts, not taking her eyes from the board.

The planchette begins to move again. F-R-E-E-D-O-M

Emma smiles. 'Thank you,' she says.

She looks relieved, and seems happier for her message. The look of fear has gone, her face has relaxed and she continues to smile. I find myself feeling a bit more relaxed. I'm not sure if it's Emma's sudden calmness or the whiskey, but I suddenly feel pretty good about this. It will be a good story to tell.

'Do you have any more messages?' Zach.

Yes. Z-A-C-H-A-R-Y

'Go on,' he says.

S-W-I-M-L-I-K-E-A-F-I-S-H

This one needs no explanation. Zach swims for the county and he has a big race coming up in a couple of weeks. He smiles. 'Thank you, I will.'

Scurra doesn't wait for the questions anymore. The planchette moves off of its own accord.

K-A-Y-L-E-I-G-H

I'm suddenly nervous. What if my message is a bad one? I needn't have worried.

Y-O-U-A-R-E-M-Y-F-A-V-O-U-R-I-T-E

'Thank you Scurra,' I say beaming. I notice a frown fleetingly cross Zach's face. It leaves as quickly as it came. Maybe I imagined it? No, it was definitely there. I make a mental note to ask him about it later.

We expectantly for Kev's message, but the planchette merely sits there.

'Do you have a message for me?' asks Kev.

Yes.

No more movement. This is getting weird. I have a bad feeling about this. It's as though Scurra doesn't want to give Kev his message. It must be bad!

'Please tell me,' says Kev, no note of worry in his voice or expression. I want to tell him not to ask. I want to jump up and break the circle, but I'm rooted to my seat, I feel like I can't move. I will myself to speak, and just as I find my voice, the planchette starts to move again. I am too late.

Y-O-U-H-A-V-E-T-H-E-A-N-S-W-E-R-W-I-T-H-I-N-Y-O-U-R-R-E-A-C-H

'What does that even mean?' asks Kev. The message seems innocent enough, but my bad feeling isn't going away.

The planchette starts to move again and I think Kev will get his message explained like Emma did. I am wrong. It spins out of control, and flies across the room, missing the TV by inches. A small scream escapes me.

'Guess they left,' says Zach, breaking the tension, and I laugh at my fear.

'Does that always happen at the end then?' I ask.

'Dunno, that's the first time I've got it to work.'

Before I can question him further, Emma speaks up 'It gave us all what we wanted most in the world. Zach wants to win his swim meet, Kayleigh has a need to be liked and Kev likes to be the one who knows everything.'

I think this assessment of us might be a little harsh. It makes me sound needy and it makes Kev sound like an arrogant know-it-all. It doesn't change the fact it's true though. I do have a need to be liked and Kev likes to be the problem solver.

'What about you,' I demand, a little sharper than I meant to. Emma bringing up my need to be liked had definitely touched a nerve. I force my tone to be more reasonable. 'You're hardly a prisoner are you?'

'Maybe not in the sense of jail, but you know how strict my mum is since dad left. I would sure love a little more freedom at times.'

I nod. I get it. Emma's mum is pretty strict. She's only here tonight because she lied to her and told them we were at my house. No way would she have allowed her to be at a boy's house. Especially with his parents out.

Zach goes and retrieves the planchette, puts it back in the box, and folds the board away, also adding that to the box. Watching him, I remember I wanted to ask him about his frown.

'Since when did you want to be Mr. Popular Zach, I thought you couldn't care less whether or not people liked you?' I keep it light.

'Huh?'

'When I got my message you frowned. You tried to hide it, but I saw you.'

'I don't want to be popular. It was something else.'

'Care to elaborate?'

'Not really.'

He picks up the box and goes to walk towards the door.

'Oh come on,' I say and he stops and turns back to us.

'Look, it's probably not a big deal ok. The spirit gave us all nice messages. It's probably a nice spirit.'

I wait for him to go on and that sense of dread creeps back in. He fiddles with his shirt.

'It's just, well, you, well, you said the spirit's name.'

'So?' I feel like I'm missing something important here.

'Just people say by using its name you give it power. You open up the door to let it in.'

I relax. I don't know what I was expecting, but it wasn't some superstitious old wives' tale.

'Yeah, I'm not worried,' I say. When he doesn't move or respond, I continue, more to reassure him than me. 'It was a nice spirit. You said so yourself. Anyway, it's obviously gone now.'

He snaps himself out of it. 'Yeah.'

'We should go, it's getting kinda late,' says Kev, checking his watch.

'Ok, let's just clean this mess up first,' I say gesturing to the broken glass and whiskey.

'You go ahead, I'll do that,' says Emma, throwing me a grin. She's back to her usual self.

'Ok,' I agree. Normally I would have insisted on helping, but it's obvious she wants some alone time with Zach.

'See you both tomorrow at my party!'

I hug Zach and Emma and Kev hugs Emma and gives Zach a clap on the shoulder. 'Catch you all tomorrow.'

I'm walking along the street towards the shopping centre where I am meeting Emma. The sun is beating down and I'm glad I didn't wear a coat. I feel like skipping, and I can hardly keep the grin from my face.

Last night keeps trying to force its way in, but I refuse to let it. It was stupid, we had drunk too much and probably shouldn't have done it. That was it. Nothing more. And I won't allow the memory of it to destroy tonight.

Today is my nineteenth birthday. My party tonight is going to be epic! Months of careful planning have gone into it and its all set. I've found the perfect dress and shoes and now I'm off into town to get my hair done. All my exams are behind me and more importantly, Kev will be there! Tonight's the night we are going to, you know, have sex (there I said it) for the first time. Life really couldn't get any better.

I am jerked rudely back to reality by a beeping horn. I jump back onto the curb, cursing under my breath. My mind drifts back to Zach saying how crossing roads aren't dangerous when you know the rules, and then Emma saying. Oh never mind. I'm not thinking about that remember.

The sun on my face makes me feel like Mother Nature is celebrating with me. I want to spread my arms, tilt my face into it and spin, but I don't. The last thing I need is becoming known as the town loony, and in a small town like ours, that wouldn't be so hard.

I arrive at the shopping centre, and pull the door open. The coolness of the air conditioning hits me. It feels good against my skin after the heat outside.

I walk towards the salon where Emma is waiting for me. I am late as usual. Normally this would put her in a bad mood but today's my birthday so she can't be mad at me.

She sees me approaching and smiles widely. 'Happy Birthday,' she says, pulling me into a hug.

'Thank you,' I smile.

My good mood must be rubbing off on her, she can't stop smiling.

'What,' I ask, my grin matching hers.

'I just got a text off Zach. He wants us to go to your party together.' She thrusts her phone into my hand. 'Read it!'

I glance down at the phone and noticing she hasn't replied, I look up at her questioningly.

'Didn't want to seem too keen,' she shrugs.

'Just answer him already.' I laugh handing the phone back to her.

She types out a message, her fingers dancing over the keys at an alarming rate. Emma is the texting queen.

'Sorted,' she announces, putting her phone in her pocket.

'About time,' I respond, rolling my eyes.

Zach and Emma have been into each other since I introduced them a month or two ago, when Kev and I first started dating. Zach is Kev's best friend and this couldn't have worked out better.

Last night seems to have brought them closer, so maybe something good is coming from it after all. I start to think back to last night, and force my thoughts away from it, forcing my mind to drift off, picturing the fun double dates we will have, long summer days spent laughing and having fun. The full summer holidays span out ahead of us. College broke up yesterday and we now have what feels like months of freedom before uni starts. There is so much to cram in, so many things we have planned. It's going to be a good summer.

I realise I've drifted away again as Emma's voice pulls me back to reality. 'You're one to talk. You and Kev have been seeing each other almost two months and you haven't even slept together yet.'

'I don't want him to think I'm easy!' I retort. It's true, but it's a little more than that. I really like Kev and I want him to stick around. I want to know he's after more than just that. The fact he has been willing to wait so long convinces me he's in it for the long haul too. I mean don't get me wrong, we've done stuff, just not that. Not yet.

Emma will never understand. She doesn't care what anyone thinks, and if she's not in bed with Zach before tonight is out, she will consider the date a failure. That's assuming it didn't happen after me and Kev left last night. 'Tonight's the night.' My grin is back.

She laughs. 'I hope he's worth the wait.'

'I know he will be. He's the one. How could he not be worth waiting for?'

'Come on,' Emma says, rolling her eyes, 'we're going to be late for your appointment,'

We head into the salon. It's busy, and the buzz of conversation fills the air. I can smell peroxide and it stings my nose a little. We announce our arrival at reception and take our seats to wait to be called over. I am going all out for the party. I've already had my nails done and a spray tan. Now there's just my hair. I'm getting it dyed blonde and re-styled.

'Kayleigh, your stylist is ready for you now,' the receptionist announces, smiling and waiting for me.

I stand up and turn around. 'Wish me luck,' I say to Emma.

'Good luck.'

I leave her flicking through a magazine and walk over to the chair the receptionist points out to me.

I explain to my stylist what I want and let her work her magic. She applies the dye, and we chat about the random things you always end up chatting about when getting your hair done.

Holidays. None for me this year. She tells me she is off to Dubai in July. Maybe I should be a little jealous, but sickening as it sounds, I would rather be here with Kev, and he can't go away this year as his mother is ill. I tell her about my upcoming party, and the time just flies by.

She rinses out the dye and starts snipping away. I try not to look; I want to see the full effect at the end.

'All done, what do you think?'

I look up and meet my bright green eyes in the mirror. I take in every detail of my hair. The new colour looks amazing with my tan, the loose curls and the side swept fringe sits perfectly. I couldn't be happier with it.

I tell her as much and she looks a little relieved. 'The blonde is such a big difference, I was a little worried you would regret it,' she says.

'I love it,' I smile back at her.

No regrets. No worries. No fears. I am happy, truly happy, for the first time in ages. Nothing is going to change that. This is my year. I just know it.

I go back to reception and pay, then walk back over to where Emma is sitting. Engrossed in her phone as usual, she doesn't look up as I approach.

I clear my throat theatrically, and she does look up. 'Wow, you look amazing.'

I smile. Emma has always been the pretty one. I'm the funny one, but maybe I can be the pretty one as well. At least for today.

* * *

'The taxi's here, come on,' my mum shouts up the stairs.

'Coming,' I shout back, grabbing my bag from the bed as I head to the door of my bedroom.

I stop in front of the full length mirror and eye myself critically, turning this way and that. I scrub up well, even if I do say so myself. At five foot three, I'm quite short, but in my new silver heels, I look a lot taller.

My dress, cream coloured with cute little pinky orange flowers sits at just the right place to be short but not too short. It is soft, flowy and screams summer. My hair curls just right, and sits atop my shoulders, the length hanging down my chest, my fringe sweeping just above my left eye. My eyes sparkle.

I can't stop smiling as I look at the necklace Kev bought me for my birthday. It is silver, my favourite, and sits just above my cleavage, catching the light as I move and sparkling, almost alive. I look good, being in love suits me.

'Kayleigh!' mum shouts.

I give myself one last spritz of perfume and make for the door, heading down to the waiting taxi.

'You look stunning,' says my mum, proudly.

'Thanks Mum,' I say.

My dad turns from where he is locking the door, and looks at me. 'Hmmm, maybe a little too stunning. Be careful tonight, Kayleigh.'

'Dad, I'm going to be at a party with you there, what can go wrong?'

'It's after the party I'm worried about, when you go off with him.'

I roll my eyes. 'Whatever Dad,' I say. As I think of Kev, I feel a small smile playing across my lips.

'What?' asks mum, smiling herself.

'Just happy,' I say, and it's not a lie. I am happy.

Finally, we are all in the taxi. Me, mum, dad and Shaun, my little brother. At eleven he's not so little anymore, he's as tall as me and shows no signs of stopping growing.

The taxi pulls away from the curb and heads towards my local where the party is taking place.

I feel another wave of excitement roll through my stomach. Even dad's over protectiveness can't burst my bubble tonight. I know he actually quite likes Kev, he just worries about me. It's a dad's job to worry I suppose, but with Kev, he has nothing to worry about. He's the perfect gentleman. He's never rushed me, he says if this is forever, a week or two won't make any difference. I think that makes me love him even more if that's even possible.

We pull up outside the pub, and as dad pays the taxi, I see Kev stood waiting for me. The sight of him makes me catch my breath a little. He is wearing blue jeans and a white T- shirt, but for how good he looks, it could be an Armani suit. His dark hair is ruffled slightly, just the way I like it, and the edge of his dragon tattoo is just visible below his sleeve.

The butterflies dance away in my stomach as I push open the car door and walk towards him. He pulls me in for a kiss, then pushes me back slightly, holding me by my upper arms. 'You are beautiful,' he says simply, then pulls me back to him for another kiss.

As our lips meet, I put my arms around his back, feeling the taut muscle under his T-shirt. I feel the warmth spread down from my stomach and I melt as his lips move with mine.

'Ok, that's enough, put her down.'

Dad's voice reminds me where I am, and I pull back, clearing my throat.

'Hey, Mr Pearson,' Kev smiles, seemingly unruffled, although I notice he looks a little flushed.

'I think it's time you called us by our first names, seeing as you and my daughter are now joined at the mouth,' dad says. He tries to appear stern, but his smile is already spreading. 'I'm Peter and this is Kathy.' He gestures towards mum.

'Sure,' said Kev, smiling at first dad, then mum. 'My dad sends his apologies, but he just didn't feel comfortable leaving my mum alone.'

His smile fades a little at the mention of his mum and my heart breaks for him. She has terminal cancer and she only has a few months left. I reach out and give his hand a little squeeze. He squeezes back and doesn't let go.

'Let's go before this gets really gross,' says Shaun, always so melodramatic. I am grateful that he's broken the tension a little.

We walk in and Kev and dad head for the bar, while mum, Shaun and I take our seats. I choose the table nearest the door, after all I have to greet guests as they arrive.

We are the first to arrive. I feel the first prick of nerves trying to burst my happy bubble. What if no one shows up? I tell myself to calm down. The invites said 7.30 and its only just after 7. I purposely arrived early, just in case anything needed doing.

I look around the room properly for the first time. The DJ is all set up, and puts on some music, now he notices we have arrived. The buffet table is all set up and the food looks lovely. Banners and balloons are everywhere I look and with the flashing disco lights making patterns across the dance floor, the room looks perfect. Mum has done me proud with the decorating, that's for sure.

Kev is back from the bar. He hands me my vodka and coke, and I take a long drink. That will calm my nerves.

I excuse myself and go to the toilet to reapply my lipstick and check my hair. I take a deep breath and head back towards our table. As I do, the first of my guests arrive. Some friends from college.

Eagerly I go over and greet them. They are a little giggly. They must have had a few drinks while getting ready. Why didn't I think of that?

'We came early because the waiting for people to show up is the worst part isn't it,' one of them, I think it was Clare, says.

I nod, relieved, as they thrust cards and gift bags into my hands, and head off to the bar in a whirl of excited chatter and laughter.

There was definitely some truth to Emma saying I have a need to be liked. I do. I don't know why. I used to try to be more like her, and not care what people think, but I've given up on that. I'm a people pleaser, it's just the way I am.

I reach our table and unload the bags. As I go to re-take my seat, more people come in. I breathe a sigh of relief. Maybe the people pleasing has paid off.

The night flies by in a blur of greetings, conversations, dancing and laughter. I have caught up with family and some old friends, spending the night flitting from table to table, exchanging brief conversations so I can get round everyone. I am in my element.

I've cut my cake, made the obligatory cringy speech, and drank far too many shots of tequila. I've finally made it to the dance floor. I'm happily in the moment, dancing, when I feel a hand slide onto my hip. I turn and my eyes meet Kev's.

'I've hardly seen you all night, dance with me,' he says, slipping his arms around me. As if the DJ has read our minds, he puts on How Long Will I Love You. I silently mouth the words, my eyes locked on Kev's. He leans in and kisses me, and in that moment it's like we are the only two people in the world. I feel a surge of desire like I've never felt before, and I have to pull back from his kiss. I catch my breath, and rest my head on his shoulder for the remainder of the song.

All too soon it is over. People are coming up to say their goodbyes. Kev kisses my cheek. 'Its fine,' he smiles, sensing my feeling that I am neglecting him a little. 'This is your night, enjoy it. Our time is coming.' He winks, and a jolt of electricity runs through my body.

As the last of the guests leave, I realise I didn't say good bye to Emma. I walk back to our table where my family and Kev are waiting for me to finish saying goodbye to the stragglers. 'Anyone know what happened to Emma?' I ask.

Shaun pulls a face of disgust, his mouth curling down. 'She left. With a boy. They were kissing.' He mimes throwing up.

Kev laughs. 'She and Zach left a while ago. She said to tell you she'd call you tomorrow. They seemed pretty happy.'

I smile. For all Zach is a bit of a joker at times, he's a good guy deep down and I think him and Emma will be perfect together.

'Our taxi is here,' dad announces to mum and Shaun, after checking his phone. They start to gather up all my cards and presents. They are going to take them home for me so I can stay with Kev. Dad turns to me. 'I hope you enjoyed the party.'

'Oh, I did. Thank you both so much.' I hug him and mum in turn. I think of hugging Shaun too, but decide against it – it would only embarrass him. I ruffle his hair instead, and he pulls away, his face reddening. I smile.

'Enjoy the rest of your night. Be careful, and I'll see you tomorrow,' says dad.

He turns to Kev. 'Look after her.'

'Of course,' answers Kev.

Kev helps mum and dad load the presents into the car, and we begin the short walk to his house, laughing and chatting. I'm so happy I barely feel the ache in my feet and the chill in the air.

We arrive at Kev's, and he takes me by the hand, leading me through the house and out into the back garden. We walk to the bottom of the garden and into the converted stables. Kev is so lucky he has his own space. The stables have been converted into a bedroom/lounge with a kitchenette and a shower room.

Kev only got this because his mother is so ill and his dad felt it was unfair to him to be forced to live in a house that is more hospital than home. It must be hard for him and I'm glad he has somewhere to come to get away from it. I'm also glad we have somewhere we can truly be alone.

I wish I had something like this. I feel a pang of guilt thinking this.

I must have shown my guilt on my face. Kev stops with the key still in the lock unturned. 'What is it?' he asks.

'Nothing,' I answer. 'I just feel a bit guilty letting mum and dad lug all my presents home.'

'They want you to enjoy your night, stop worrying,' he says, unlocking the door.

I nod. I know I shouldn't lie to him but I could hardly tell him what I was really thinking.

Kev pushes the door open for me and I step inside. He follows, locking the door behind us.

I step out of my shoes, as Kev turns from the door, and looks over at me. I am suddenly nervous. I swallow and look at the ground, my fingers coming together and twiddling.

Kev closes the distance between us and tilting my chin up, kisses me gently. 'If you don't want to, I understand.'

The nerves vanish, and I kiss him hungrily, urgently, my tongue finding his, my hands sliding under his T-shirt, feeling his warm skin against mine. He pushes one hand into my hair, the other pulling me tightly against him.

I pull back long enough to wrestle his T-shirt over his head. I lean back in, and he kisses down my neck, passionate, hungry for me. He pulls down the zipper on my dress and I let it fall to the floor, the material sliding over my skin, igniting every nerve ending as it goes, then kicking it away.

I reach for his button and undo his jeans, pushing them and his boxers down his thighs. As he bends down to remove his shoes and socks and pull his jeans the rest of the way off, I reach behind me and unhook my bra, throwing it down on the increasing pile of clothes.

He stands back up, turning me to face away from him and pulling me against him, one hand teasing my nipples, the other pushes down my panties and he slowly rubs my clitoris. I kick my panties away. All my senses are alive and I feel like I am about to explode. I can feel his erection pressing up against me and I want to feel him inside me now.

I arch my back and he kisses my neck, and along my collar bone. My breathing quickens.

I reach behind me, my fingers tracing lazy circles on his stomach and thighs, teasing him.

He increases the pressure on my clit, and I thrust my hips hungrily against his hand, my breath catching. I feel my climax building like a wave inside me.

My hand encircles his hard cock, moving up and down and he lets outs a moan. 'Kayleigh,' he says breathily against my neck, and I know I can't hold off much longer, I am throbbing with pleasure, and I can feel how wet I am.

Kev's urgency matches my own, and wrapping his hand once more in my hair, he pushes my head forward, bending me towards his couch's back, spreading me open. I reach out my hands, clutching the edge of his couch, steadying myself as he pushes his length inside me in one hard thrust. I moan gently.

Holding my hips, he pushes himself in deeper, deeper, and I feel him stretch me, fill me, and I can't think straight, can't think of anything but him and the way he feels thrusting inside me, pulling me back to meet his thrusts.

He thrusts faster and faster, and I gasp, I can't hold back any longer. The climax hits me hard, washing over me in a rush of warmth, spreading through my entire body. I feel my vagina clench around him over and over, as I ride the wave of ecstasy. My legs go weak, like jelly, and if he wasn't holding me, I would fall.

His breathing is getting faster and as my vagina clenches once more around him, I feel his muscles tenses, and feel the warm rush of his orgasm drench my insides, his cock twitching, moaning my name.

I feel him pull out of me, and for a second I feel cold, empty. I straighten up, my legs still a little shaky, and turn to him. 'Wow,' he breathes, pulling me to him and holding me close.

I feel his chest rise and fall as he catches his breath. 'Yes, wow,' I agree.

Stepping out of our embrace, he pulls the couch back straight, a smile spreading across his face as he does so.

He leads me to his bed, pulling back the duvet, and I climb in, turning to face him as he climbs in beside me. I put my head on his chest, just below his shoulder, my hand on his stomach, and he puts his arms around me, holding me tightly.

'I love you Kayleigh,' he says after a few minutes.

'I love you too,' I reply, and I do. I really do.

We lay in comfortable silence, and I can't keep the smile from my face. I feel his arms slacken and his breathing becomes slower and deeper as he drifts off to sleep, and I know I should let him sleep, but I'm not ready for this night to end yet.

I push myself up and straddle his hips. His eyes flutter open and he smiles sleepily as I rub my still wet lips along the length of his hardening cock. I reach behind me, lifting myself and slip him back inside me.

I lower my body, impaling myself on his length, and begin moving up and down, slowly, teasing him, each movement pushing him further up me. He reaches out with one hand, and presses against my clitoris, his fingers circling, probing, and rubbing.

I begin to move faster, matching the rhythm of his fingers against me, and I feel another wave building. I orgasm even harder this time, my whole body is alive with heat, every nerve ending screaming out, my back arching involuntarily as the orgasm takes over my body. My lips part and a strangled 'Aaaah' escapes me, as my juices flood over him.

As the orgasm fades, I move harder, faster, and Kev's hips thrust with me. His hands are fisting in the sheets either side of me, one of them slick and shiny with my wetness. With one final thrust, he cums hard, his juices mixing with mine, his face contorted in a mix of pain and pleasure.

He stills and I climb off him, curling back in to his side. I feel the heat of his skin against mine, and I tilt my head up to kiss him as our breathing returns to normal.

'You trying to wear me out already?' he laughs.

'Oh no,' I reply, 'I want you in prime condition.'

I settle against him, encircled in his arms, feeling his pleasure trickling out of me. I feel warm, safe, loved, and I've never been happier.

'I hope you enjoyed your birthday,' he mumbles, his voice slurred with oncoming sleep.

I smile 'It was the best birthday ever,' I respond, kissing his chest.

As I drift into sleep, Kev snoring gently beside me, I know I was telling the truth. It really was the best birthday ever.

Chapter Three

The last few weeks have passed in a blur. A fast paced, happy blur, but a blur all the same. Kev and I have been for days out, picnics in the park, nights at our favourite bars and clubs, and cosy nights in. Zach and Emma are still going strong too and we have been out as a foursome a fair few times. Sometimes I have to pinch myself. It all seems a little too perfect.

The only downside to it all is Kev's mum has been going gradually downhill. I know he is upset about it, but he puts on a brave face, and I think deep down he thinks it will be a relief for her to be out of pain at last.

It's going to be time to start uni before I know it. Only six more weeks. I got accepted at my first choice and even better I just found out Kev also got accepted. I was a little worried that being apart for so long would cause us problems. Now we aren't going to be apart. The four of us are heading out tonight for drinks to celebrate.

It's going to be a double celebration. Our uni acceptance and Zach winning his swim meet. That might be a little presumptuous as he isn't actually swimming until this afternoon, but he is good, really good, so it's a pretty safe bet.

I am sat on the bottom stair slipping my shoes on as the doorbell goes.

'It's open,' I call out. The door opens and in bounces Emma, an explosion of energy.

'Do I look ok? What do you even wear to a swim meet? Especially when you are going out afterwards,' she rattles off not leaving a gap for me to answer.

'Relax,' I laugh. 'You look great.'

She does look great, in a light pink sundress and white flip flops, she looks like the queen of summer. Her straight black hair sits just above her shoulders and she fiddles with it, fluffing it up.

I look down at my own outfit – a yellow halter neck top, denim hot pants and wedges. Now I feel under dressed. I shake off the feeling. It's the swimming pool followed by the local, I hardly need to be rocking a Chanel gown.

'You ready?' asks Emma, keen to be on the move.

'Yep,' I reply standing up and smoothing out my top. I grab a bobble and twist my hair into a loose ponytail. Grabbing my bag, I make for the door.

'See ya,' I shout.

'Bye,' comes the response as the door closes.

'You're so lucky,' says Emma, 'my mum gives me the third degree on where I'm going, who I'm with, what time will I be back. I swear she thinks I'm still about twelve.'

'It's only because she cares,' I respond automatically. Actually I imagine this would get really annoying really quickly.

'Whatever,' Emma responds, sounding unconvinced. 'I can't wait to get to uni, it's going to be brilliant having some freedom.'

I feel cold all over. My skin breaks out in goose bumps despite the heat of the afternoon sun. Freedom. That was Emma's message the night we did the Ouija board.

I shake my head slightly to clear it. Where did that come from. I haven't thought about it since the day of the party. It was a game. Just a game.

And would it really be so bad if Emma got her freedom?

Emma glances at me, her stream of chatter stopping abruptly. 'Are you even listening?'

'Sorry, a goose walked over my grave.' Why did I use the word grave?

'Get a grip,' I tell myself as Emma watches me out of the corner of her eye.

'Zach is going to be brilliant today,' I say, as we approach the pool, lightening the mood and getting Emma talking again so she can stop scrutinising me.

'I know, have you ever seen him swim?'

'No, but I've heard he's good.'

'Oh, he is. And he looks so fit when he's all wet and glistening,' Emma adds, a twinkle in her eye.

'You have a one track mind,' I laugh.

She nods. 'I know. You would too if you had been on a three-day sex ban. Stupid coach, just because he isn't getting any, he thinks we all should suffer.'

I can't help but laugh at how dramatic Emma is.

We arrive at the pool, go inside and take our seats a couple of rows from the front. It's lovely and cool. I look around. It's a good turn out, and a lot of the people there have banners with Zach's name on them.

'Hey,' says Kev, sliding into the seat beside me.

'Hi,' respond Emma and I simultaneously. He laughs.

We chat for a few minutes about our plans for the night.

'We need to do lots of shots,' Emma announces. She gets no arguments.

The door to the side of the pool opens and the swimmers emerge and begin doing stretches. The crowd are waving their banners and chanting. It's a good atmosphere, and I can feel myself getting caught up in it.

Zach looks up and spots us. Smiling, he saunters over from the side of the pool, and kisses Emma. 'Hi,' he says to me and Kev.

'Good luck,' I say, feeling like a bit of a groupie.

'Well, I best get moving,' he says. 'Can't keep the coach waiting.'

He goes back to join the rest of his team, removing his track suit. The swimmers hop in the water, swimming a few strokes to warm up.

At the sound of a whistle, they all climb out of the pool. Most of them go to stand pool side by their respective coaches. The swimmers in the first race walk around to take their starting places. The first race is the 500M, one of Zach's. The one he has been tipped to beat the current record in.

There are several scouts here and I know he must be nervous, but he hides it really well, the picture of confident up there.

Emma is practically swooning, making appreciative noises, her face shining.

The man with the whistle gives a quick run-down of the rules.

'Take your marks,' he shouts. 'Set.'

'Here wo go, give it all you've got baby,' says Emma, too quiet for Zach to hear, but loud enough to make me and Kev smile.

The swimmers are poised, ready to jump on his command.

'GO!'

They all jump into the pool and begin swimming. The cheers go up all around us and we jump to our feet joining in enthusiastically.

'Go Zach,' I scream.

The swimmers start emerging back up from their initial dives, cutting through the water so fast they are like blurs, water splashing left right and centre.

'Where is he?' Emma asks impatiently, her camera at the ready.

'He can go a long way under water, have a bit of faith,' responds Kev jokingly.

I smile, but suddenly I am hit by a wave of nervous nausea. Something isn't right. He's been down there too long. I feel a rush of goose flesh run up and down my arms, and the coolness of the room suddenly feels too cold. I rub my arms.

I can see Zach's coach walking towards the pool, looking on anxiously.

The crowd seem to notice something is wrong as one, and they quiet down.

Time is moving in slow motion. All I can hear is the splash of water, the occasional shout and the blood pumping in my ears. It is only a couple of seconds but it feels like a lifetime.

The whistle is being blown frantically, and the swimmers are stopping and looking around as they realise something has happened.

That's when I see it. The pool of red rising in Zach's lane, followed by his limp body.

His coach and the coach of one of the opposition teams jump into the pool and swim towards him. They get a hold of him and pull him to the side where his team mates are waiting to pull him out.

I can hear Emma beside me quietly saying 'no, no, no' over and over again. I want to reach out, to comfort her but I can't move. It's like I'm watching this on a TV screen, seeing it but not really a part of it.

'Can we get some help here, he's not breathing,' shouts the coach, and his shout breaks the spell. Suddenly there is noise and movement all around me as people jump into action.

Emma leaves my side and runs down the steps to the pool side area, barging people aside in her haste to reach him. A woman screams. I think it's his mother.

I don't know what to do. There are people everywhere, some jostling about trying to see what is going on, some heading for the exits, but most, like me, stay where they are, shell shocked.

Something tickles me face and I reach up to brush it away. My hand comes away wet and I realise I am crying silent tears. I want to go to Emma, where she stands, pool side, wanting to be close to Zach but not wanting to get in the way. I can't move. I feel like my whole body has turned to lead. I am issuing commands to move, but my limbs aren't responding.

The doors Emma and I came through half an hour ago, when everything was good and no one was getting CPR, burst open, and two paramedics come running in, carrying a medical bag and a stretcher.

The crowd parts for them as they reach Zach. They get to work on him and I allow myself a glimmer of hope as they load Zach onto a stretcher. The glimmer is extinguished instantly as they pull a crisp white sheet over his face.

My knees buckle and I fall back into my seat.

'What the fuck just happened?' asks Kev from my side to no one in particular.

I shake my head. I have to get back in the moment. People need me, and I need to be there for them. I feel like I have been zoned out for hours watching the unpleasant drama unfold. In reality, it can't have been longer than seven or eight minutes.

I finally snap out of it at the sound of a noise. A hysterical wailing sound, filled with more grief and pain than I ever thought possible. The wail is primal, animalistic and it cuts through me like a knife. It is Zach's mum. His father steers her away behind the paramedic his face ashen and drawn, the face of an old man who has seen everything bad in the world.

'I need to go find Emma,' I say to Kev. He looks a little pale but otherwise ok.

'Of course,' he responds. 'I'll go get the car ready and I'll drive the two of you to her house.'

I put my hand briefly on his arm. 'Thank you,' I say.

His best friend has just died in front of him and he is still more worried about getting Emma and I out of here. We make our way around the people who are still in the seats around us. Kev turns towards the exit, and I stop him, putting my arms around him and hugging him tightly. He squeezes me back. I am torn. I want to be there for Kev but Emma needs me too.

'I'm ok, go get Emma,' he says, giving me an out. At this moment, Emma is in more of a state. He's right, I need to go to her. I nod and Kev turns to the exit again, and I let him walk away this time.

I walk down the stairs, seeing Emma straight away, I make my way over to her. I am expecting her to be crying, screaming, and cursing the world. She isn't. She is stood perfectly still, one strap of her dress hanging off her shoulder and her hair all over. She looks like a lost child, and my heart aches for her.

'Emma,' I say, pulling her into a hug. 'I'm so sorry.'

She is stiff in my arms, neither pushing me away nor hugging me back. I release her and stand back a little.

'Emma?'

I reach out and push her hair out of her eyes. Still she makes no sign she has even seen me. Her eyes are glassy and it's like she's looking at something no one else can see. I push her strap back onto her shoulder.

'Let's get you home.' I say, because I can think of nothing else. I take her elbow and gently propel her forwards. She allows herself to be lead up the stairs, out of the door and into the parking lot.

As I scan the cars looking for Kev, she finally speaks. So quiet I would think I had imagined it if not for her lips moving.

'What am I supposed to do without him K?'

I have no idea what to say to that. I am not one of those people who knows what to say in these situations. Emma was always the one who said all the right things, while I stood off to the side looking awkward.

'You'll get through this,' I finally manage. A cliché I know and not enough. Not nearly enough.

'I guess I'll have to, won't I,' she says, a thin smile crossing her mouth. It looks so out of place on her otherwise expressionless face.

As I desperately try to think of what to say next, Kev pulls up in front of us. I open the back door and Emma climbs in. Looking straight ahead she makes no move to close the door. I push it shut and climb into the front passenger seat.

Kev is saying something to Emma that I don't catch. She doesn't respond, just continues staring straight ahead. Kev looks at me, one eyebrow raised questioningly, and I shake my head slightly. I have no idea what to do.

'Let's just get her home,' I say.

Kev nods, and putting the car into drive, he pulls out of the car park.

A few minutes later, we pull up outside Emma's house. None of us have spoken a word.

'Stay here while I go and have a quick word with your mum,' I say to Emma. She makes no indication she has heard me but she doesn't go to exit the car.

'I won't be long,' I say to Kev. 'I'm going to try and explain what happened.'

'Want me to come?' he asks.

I shake my head. 'No, I think you should stay with her.'

He nods agreement, and I get out of the car, walk up Emma's path and ring her door bell. I have walked that path so many times, rang that doorbell so many times, but never has each step felt so heavy.

Emma's mum answers.

'Kayleigh!' she exclaims. 'Emma isn't here, I thought she was with you.'

'She was. She is,' I stammer. 'Can I come in for a second?'

'Of course dear. You look terrible. What happened? Is Emma ok?'

She stands back and I step into the passage way and into the kitchen. Once so familiar it seems like a stranger's place now. Nothing will ever feel the same again.

I haltingly explain to Karen everything that has happened at the swim meet. As the story continues, she pales a little and reaching out to the breakfast bar, she sits on a stool.

'Now she is barely speaking and we didn't know what to do,' I finish.

Karen gets a hold of herself, and composed once more, she stands up and places her hand on my arm.

'You did the right thing getting her out of there and bringing her home,' she says. 'I told her that boy was trouble, that he would break her heart. She thinks I'm too strict but maybe now she will see I was right.'

I am too shocked to speak for a second. I can't believe Karen is using this as an "I told you so" moment.

I find my voice.

'With all due respect Karen, he didn't cheat on her, or hurt her by choice. He died.' I choke slightly on the word died.

'Well now I'm not implying he did it on purpose, I'm just saying that maybe now she will listen to me about getting too involved with boys.'

'Are you for real? God, then you wonder why I don't want to be around you! I just need some freedom Mum.' Emma. I'm glad she is responding normally again, but I fear that her hearing what her Mother just said isn't going to help either of them.

I turn and see her standing in the door way with Kev.

'Emma,' starts Karen.

'Just leave me alone,' Emma shouts, turning and running for the stairs, her voice breaking.

I go to follow her, but Karen stops me.

'Thank you for bringing her home Kayleigh, I'll take it from here. I think I may have been a little hard on her. I will let her calm down a little then go and have a talk to her. Can you see yourself out?'

'Yes,' I respond, obviously dismissed. 'Will you have her call me when she feels up to it?'

'Of course, thanks again.'

Once we are back in the car, Kev turns to me.

'I'm sorry, she just opened the door and made a dash for it. I didn't really try to stop her, I figured she needed her mum.'

'It's fine,' I say. 'It's not your fault. Actually, Karen isn't usually that bad. She's strict sure, but she's not totally insensitive, I think she was just shocked.'

Kev doesn't look convinced but he lets it go.

'I don't think I want to go out anymore, want to come hang out at mine for a bit?' he asks.

'Yeah,' I reply. I don't want to even think about going out. Truth be told I want to go home, go to my room and be alone, but I don't think Kev should be alone right now. He is more upset than he is showing and I want to be there for him.

I take my phone out and text my mum telling her I'm staying at Kev's. I'll explain the rest tomorrow. She'll only worry if I try and explain now. In hindsight, I'm not sure how I thought she wouldn't hear about what happened. I guess I'm more shaken than I want to admit.

*   *   *

I open my eyes. The sun is pouring in and Kev is just starting to stir beside me. I stretch, and yawn lazily. That's how long it takes for the events of yesterday to catch back up with me.

After arriving back at Kev's place, we sat in silence for a while, both of us staring at, but not watching a movie. We talked, but we both carefully avoided talking about what had happened. We will have to talk about it at some point, but not that night. It was too raw. Too real. I was relieved when he started yawning and asked if I was ready for bed. It is exhausting avoiding the one thing you need to talk about but don't want to acknowledge.

Kev slips his arm around me and kisses my shoulder, bringing me back to the present and I turn to face him.

'Morning,' he says. 'How are you doing?'

'I'll be ok,' I say. 'You?'

He shrugs. 'I guess it hasn't really hit me yet, but yeah, I'll be ok too.'

'I need to call Emma,' I say.

He stands up out of bed. 'Give her a call while I take a shower,' he says, 'then I'll drive you over there.'

'Thanks,' I say, reaching for my phone as he leaves the room.

My call goes straight to her voicemail, so I tap out a text: Call me ASAP, I need to know you're ok.

I put my phone on the bed beside me and stand up, walking towards the window. The door opens and Kev comes back in.

'That was quick,' I say, turning around. Seeing his expression, my stomach turns over. 'What is it, what happened?'

He pulls on a T-shirt and a pair of boxers. 'You better come into the house,' he says.

'What happened?' I ask again, grabbing my own clothes and putting them on, going into autopilot mode.

'As I went to go into the shower room, I saw dad coming across the lawn. He said we need to go inside. Your parents are here.'

Mum and dad are here? I pick my phone back up and look at the screen. 11 missed calls.

I feel myself getting angry.

'Stop avoiding the question and tell me what the hell is going on,' I snap.

'I don't know how to tell you.' His voice is quiet, gentle and he looks down at the floor as he speaks.

The anger leaves as quickly as it came, replaced with a mixture of horror and fear. Something bad has happened.

'Is it Shaun?' I ask.

'No,' he responds quickly. 'Shaun is fine.'

The relief I feel doesn't last long. I'm happy Shaun is ok, but something has still happened. Something horrible.

'Please,' I whisper.

'Emma killed herself last night. I'm so sorry,' he says.

He crosses the room, and puts his arms around me as my knees go loose and I start to fall. My vision swims in and out, and suddenly I'm hot. Too hot to bear, sweat prickling my skin.

I feel the sick rising, and push Kev off, making a desperate break for the toilet. I make it just in time.

Kev comes up behind me, as I kneel over the toilet, coughing and retching, my stomach already empty. He rubs my back.

I finally stop retching, and I stand up and go to the sink, rinse my mouth, and splash a little cold water on my face.

'I don't understand,' I say.

'That's all I know. Your mum has the full story.'

'Ok,' I nod. 'Just give me a minute to compose myself.'

I close the toilet lid and sit down on it, slowing my breathing, trying to stop shaking, stop the room from spinning. Kev walks over to me and I stand up, holding onto him like a drowning person holding onto a life ring. He holds me, stroking my back, my hair, and whispering soothing words into my ear. I never want to let go, but I know I have to. I have to find out exactly what happened.

I know Emma was upset, but to kill herself? I just couldn't equate the word suicide with my larger than life, bubbly best friend. Maybe it's a sick joke. No, not that. My parents and Kev would never do that. A mistake then. Yeah, that's it. It's a mistake.

Finally, the room stops spinning and I get a little control of myself. 'Let's do this,' I say.

Kev takes my hand and leads me through the garden, through his parent's kitchen, and into their sitting room. Kev's dad stands up when we enter. He looks like he is about to speak, but then I see my mum, and it's like the floodgate opens. I throw myself into her waiting arms, and cry. I cry for Emma, for Zach, for me and Kev, for everyone and everything. I feel like I will never stop crying. Eventually I do of course.

'Tell me everything,' I say, wiping my eyes.

Chapter Four

'I received a phone call in the early hours of the morning from Karen,' my mum begins, holding my hands in hers.

'She was hysterical – the only words I caught were Emma and hospital – so I got in my car and drove over there.'

She pauses. 'Are you sure you want to hear this Kayleigh?'

I nod. Actually, I don't want to hear this, it's the last thing I want to hear. What I want is to wake up and shower away the nightmare. I know that's not going to happen. I need to know what happened to my best friend.

Taking a moment, she continues. 'By the time I got there, Karen seemed to have calmed down a little. She was drinking whiskey, and who could blame her. I asked her if Emma was ok.

''Emma is dead,' she replied.'

'Dead!' I exclaimed. Part of me had hoped that somehow Kev had gotten it wrong, that she attempted to kill herself, a cry for help, and they got to her in time. They saved her.

'Yes. Suicide.

'Karen told me Emma asked her to pop out to the shops and get her some headache tablets. When she returned, she could see as she drove up to the house that one of the upstairs windows was wide open.

'She said Emma was lying there in the driveway in a pool of blood, and she ran to her, pulling her mobile phone out and calling for an ambulance as she did. She sat holding her hand, begging her to wake up, but she didn't. The ambulance arrived and confirmed what she already knew.

'The police arrived and escorted Karen inside. That's when she found the note. The police have it now, but Karen said you can see it once it is returned.

'She was sat at the kitchen counter when I arrived. I don't think she had moved from that moment until the moment she called me.'

'What did the note say?' I ask, though I'm sure I can guess after what happened to Zach. I imagine it was Kev and not Zach. Would I want to live without him? I really don't know.

'Karen remembered it word for word, and now I do too. I guess that sort of stuff doesn't leave you. It said: 'Sorry mum, I don't want to live anymore – I need to have my freedom. I want to fly like a bird.' Kayleigh are you alright?'

I feel the colour leave my face, the room spinning alarmingly, but I nod. Fly like a bird. Freedom. Something isn't right here.

'That's all we know at the minute,' my mum continues, studying me intently. 'Karen is going to call when she has the details for the funeral.'

'You look awfully pale, let's get you home,' dad says. It's the first time he's spoken since I entered the room. I think that's where I get my awkwardness from. He never knows what to say to someone when something bad has happened either.

'No.' I shake my head. 'No. I'm staying with Kev.'

'But,' starts mum.

I interrupt. 'I need to be with him mum, he knows what I'm going through. Please'

It's true. He does know what I'm going through, but more than that, he knows what happened that night. He read the messages. He'll understand. I have to talk to him about this.

My mum looks across at Daniel, Kev's father, and he nods his head. 'She is welcome to stay here Kathy, I'll make sure she's ok.'

'Ok,' mum reluctantly agrees. It's obvious she doesn't want to let me out of her sight, and I feel a pang of guilt for not going home with her, but I need to talk to Kev. Alone. That reference to flying in Emma's note can't be a coincidence and he's the only one who will understand.

Mum and dad say their goodbyes, hugging me tightly, promising to come collect me if I change my mind. I nod distractedly. As I watch them reverse out of the driveway and pull away, I feel a hand on my arm.

'How are you doing?' Kev asks me.

I shrug, 'Ok I guess.'

All I can think of is the note, but I can hardly bring that up in front of Daniel. I look at Kev's face, searching for some sign he recognised the words too. His face gives nothing away. I'm trying to work out a polite way to get Kev alone when Daniel comes to my rescue.

'I need to pop out. Your mother needs some things. Will you two be ok to stay here until I get back in case your mother needs anything? I can postpone it if you need me to.'

'We're fine dad, you go,' says Kev.

He nods, and slowly gathers up his keys and wallet, watching us.

'Your mother is still sleeping; I'll be back before she wakes up.' He left the rest unsaid. The part that meant we had to stay in the house in case she wakes up early because she's in so much pain. Or worse, that she doesn't wake up at all.

As soon as the front door shuts, I round on Kev. 'You heard it right? The note. You know what that means?'

'Of course,' he responds. 'She was more upset than any of us thought.'

'But the words – freedom, flying like a bird.'

Kev interrupts me. 'You can't blame her mother for this K. I'm sure that's not what she meant. I think she meant it more as she needed to be free from the pain of losing Zach.'

'It's the message she got from the Ouija board,' I say quietly, watching my fingers pull at a piece of skin near my nail.

'Look at me Kayleigh.' I can't quite bring myself to meet his eye. Gently, he pushes my chin up, meeting my eyes. 'This is nothing to do with that.'

'How can you not see it,' I say. 'It's exactly what he said to her.'

I want to shout and scream, make him see what I can see but I can't. I can't wake his mother.

'Maybe the words were fresh in her mind because of that, maybe that's why she chose to word it the way she did. We will never know. But she didn't kill herself because of a dumb Ouija board we did over a month ago. She did that because Zach died.'

That's when the full truth hits me. How did I not see it before?

'Oh my God Kev,' I breathe. 'Zach's message was swim like a fish, and he drowned.'

'Kayleigh, it was an accident.'

'How does a star swimmer drown in a pool?' I ask.

'Listen to me,' Kev says firmly. 'You've got to let this go. Zach had a freak accident, and Emma couldn't handle it. That's it. The rest is just coincidence, and your mind is looking for a way to make sense of something senseless.'

When he puts it like that, it's hard to argue the point. Of course my theory is ridiculous. I still can't shake it off though. Something doesn't feel right about this whole thing.

'Please Kayleigh, let it go. Its crazy talk and I, I can't lose you as well.'

I realise then how selfish I've been. Kev has lost two of his best friends as well, and somehow I have made this all about me.

'You'll never lose me,' I respond, reaching out and touching his face.

'So you'll let this nonsense go?' he asks gently.

I nod. I have to, for him. He's right, it's crazy talk.

He pulls me into his arms and holds me tightly, and I squeeze back. It'll all be ok. As long as we have each other.

Even as I think the words, I know they aren't true. I can't let this go. Something is happening here, something real. I will make Kev believe me before its too late. I don't know how yet, but I'll figure something out.

For now, I want to remember my best friend as she was. Happy. Laughing. Amazing. That Ouija board took her from me when it took Zach. It took them both from me. I won't let it take anything else, not my memories of them.

Chapter Five

I wake with a start, a small scream leaving my lips. I pant, trying to calm myself down. Kev rouses beside me.

'You ok?' he asks sleepily.

'I had the dream again.'

The dream. Nightmare would be much closer to the truth. It's the same every time.

Zach is standing on the starting blocks before his race, focused, ready. His eyes flicker and the irises seem oddly yellow for a second. The whistle blows. Then he's in the pool, and he doesn't come up, the blood is spreading around him. I scream, but no one can hear me. Cut to Emma, sitting in a chair by her bedroom window, looking out over the street, staring but not seeing, crying, lost in her thoughts. Her irises flicker yellow, and she stands, pushing the window open and jumping, arms spread wide, like she is trying to fly. A sickening crack and I move to look out. I see her lying on the pavement, blood spreading around her head, a sick parody of a halo, her arms and legs bent in ways arms and legs should never bend. I scream.

And that's where I always wake up, still screaming.

Kev sits up beside me, pulling me into his arms, stroking my hair, and gently rocking me.

'Why yellow?' I ask for what seems like the hundredth time. 'Why not red, the colour of danger?'

'It's just a dream Kayleigh, it doesn't mean anything.'

I nod. I know he's right, but it feels real, and it feels like there's something I'm missing. I don't push it; I don't want any more talk of me being crazy. And I don't want to make Kev mad. He hates it when I talk like this. I've brought up the Ouija board a few more times, but he keeps shutting me down. It's got the point where I hardly dare mention it because I know he'll blow up.

'Thinking about going to the funeral today has stirred it all back up, that's all. Go back to sleep,' says Kev. 'We're going to need it to get through today.'

There's no chance of that, but I lay back down and close my eyes, clinging to Kev. I have to stop being so selfish, remember he's grieving too. He holds me as he slips back into sleep.

I fight the growing tiredness. Kev's right, I need to be alert to get through today but I am so scared of having the nightmare again, I'm so scared I'm somehow losing my mind. Eventually, I can fight no more and my eyes close.

* * *

We arrive at the church. We are fifteen minutes early, and already there's a huge crowd.

'As popular in death as they were in life,' I mutter to myself. Everyone from college is here. All Zach's team mates, their class mates. Even a few of the teachers. Kev and I pass a few muted greetings with several of our mutual friends as we make our way to the doors. My parents are there waiting for us. My mum envelopes me in a hug, followed by my dad.

'How are you holding up?' asks mum.

'I'm ok,' I shrug.

'I feel like I haven't seen you since that day. You should be home with us.'

She's right, I should be home, letting my mum fuss me. That's what I need, but I can't shake the feeling that if I leave Kev, something bad will happen to one of us. He might think I'm crazy, but crazier things have already happened, and I'm not taking any chances.

'I just... .' I start.

'It's ok,' mum interrupts. 'I understand. You do whatever you need to do to get through this'

She has no idea, but it's better for her to think that I want to be around Kev more because he gets it than to even think about telling her the truth.

'Where's Shaun?' I ask, anything to avoid talking about why we are here.

'He's at Laura's.' Laura is mum's friend. 'He said he wanted to come but I didn't think it was a good idea. He didn't fight me when I said he wouldn't be coming. I think he wanted me to stop him.'

That sounds like Shaun. He's much too proud to admit he has the fears of every other 11-year-old.

I go to respond, but the church doors open and everyone starts making their way inside.

We enter the church and take our seats. The pews are already almost full.

I've never been to a joint funeral before, I didn't even know they were a thing. When mum called round Kev's and told me about it, I thought it was a stupid idea, but now I get it. It makes sense for Emma and Zach to be together in death after the way everything happened. It's a relief only having to do it once. I'm not sure I could have handled this twice.

Kev takes my hand and gives it a squeeze. I squeeze back and don't let go.

Almost three weeks we've had to wait, while the police carried out a post mortem and ruled out any foul play. As expected, Zach's death was ruled a tragic accident, and Emma's suicide. I was a bit disappointed. I hardly expected it to be ruled death by Ouija board, but I was hopeful that the coroner would find something. I don't know what, but something, anything really, that would make them see that Zach's drowning wasn't an accident and that Emma would never kill herself.

It's a long time to wait to say goodbye, a long time to hang onto the grief. I can only imagine what it's been like for their parents.

The organ strikes up and the muted chatters and whispers drop away. The families walk down the centre, the coffins before them. It's always struck me as cruel, making the family walk the aisle, everyone staring, like some sort of death parade. With both Zach and Emma coming down the aisle together, it feels like a cruel, dark imitation of a wedding.

My heart breaks for Karen. There's only been her and Emma for as long as I can remember. Maybe that's why she was so strict. She didn't want to let her go. Zach's dad has his wife on one arm, Karen on the other. I'm so glad she didn't have to do this alone. I feel my eyes fill with tears as they walk past me, and Kev tightens his grip on my hand.

They reach the front of the church and take their seats in the front pew. The coffins are placed on the stands, the flowers arranged in front of them, and the priest begins the service.

The words wash over me. The priest's voice is soothing, but I feel like the words aren't going in. As he talks, he keeps glancing behind him at the coffins. He looks unnerved. I think I am imagining it, but others seem to have noticed. Karen is glaring at him, and people are nudging each other. I look at Kev but he seems not to have noticed. He's probably nervous. He agreed to say a few words about Zach and Emma. Karen asked me to as well, but I just couldn't face it.

The priest seems to register that people are looking at him questioningly and he takes a visible breath and gets himself under control. I've never seen a priest freak out like this before, but Emma's family where quite religious, and maybe it's affecting him more because he knew her personally.

Kev gets called up. He gives a very moving speech about friendship, and how death can never truly separate us. He talks about some memories of them both, and even manages to get a few laughs. It's what Zach and Emma would have wanted. Zach, always the life and soul of the party, always the comedian. Emma always surrounded by people, lively, bubbly.

As the speech comes to a close, I could swear I see a flash of yellow in Kev's eyes. He was right. I am going mad. It's my imagination, or a reflection from the stained glass windows. I take a deep breath, trying to steady my nerves. I need to get out of here. I need some air. I am going to be sick.

Just as quickly as it came, the yellow flash is gone, as is my nausea. Mum nudges me gently. 'Are you alright?' she mouths silently. I nod. She looks at me a moment longer until she is convinced then turns her eyes back to the front.

I have just about convinced myself I imagined the whole thing, when I catch sight of the priest out of the corner of my eye. He has gone a deathly shade of grey. He saw it too. And he knows what it means.

I vow to come back here when all this is done and ask him exactly what he thinks is going on. A man of God will know what to do. I feel calm at the notion, for the first time since Zach's accident.

Kev re-takes his seat and I whisper to him 'You did amazing.'

'Thanks,' he whispers back. 'I kind of zoned out towards the end there, do you think anyone noticed.'

I shake my head, I think only me and the priest noticed, and I'm not going down that road, not here.

He breaths a small sigh of relief.

A few more people come up and say nice things about our friends. It's nice, as funerals go. The priest says a final prayer, and the organ strikes up again as we make our way out, each person stopping to shake hands with the priest and exchange platitudes with Karen and with Zach's parents.

As I approach the priest, Kev edges around me and makes a bee line for Zach's dad. I try not to attach any significance to it, I'm being paranoid. Of course he would want to talk to Zach's parents. It's just coincidence he walked away as we got to the priest.

The priest clasps my hand in his and gives it a brisk shake. I hold it a second too long. He looks at me and his expression doesn't change, but there's something in his eyes. Pity?

Worry? Fear? I don't know, but it furthers my resolve to come back and see him. Tomorrow, I decide.

I move along and catch up with Kev. We exchange a few words with Karen and move out of the way.

'What was with that priest?' asks my dad, coming up behind me. 'He looked like he'd seen a ghost.'

'Dad!' I hiss.

He looks sheepish. 'Sorry bad choice of words.'

'His name is Father Michaels, he's new here,' says Kev. So that rules out my theory of him knowing Emma personally then, but it's hardly an explanation for his behaviour. Strangely, everyone else seems to think it is.

My dad nods 'Maybe that's it then.'

We make our way to Kev's car and my parents to theirs. The families decided on a private burial. I'm glad, I don't think I could stand this much longer. At least the priest won't be at the wake.

We make our way to the wake, our final chance to say goodbye and celebrate the lives of two people, both of whom are gone long before their time. It's in our local of course, and I try not to think that just a couple of weeks ago I had my birthday party here with my best friends beside me. They had their whole lives ahead of them and now they are gone. I feel my eyes fill with tears at the thought of it.

'Hey, no crying,' Karen says sitting down beside me.

I smile. 'Sorry.'

'It's hard not to,' she agrees, 'but we agreed that the wake would be happy, a celebration of Emma and Zach.

'I wanted to talk to you about what happened when you brought Emma home that day.'

'Go on,' I encourage her. Did she notice something?

'The way I reacted was appalling. I'm so sorry. I didn't mean it the way it came out.'

'It's ok, I get it.'

She continues. 'Thank you, I'm glad you understand. I want you to know that I spoke to Emma. I apologised to her and I think she realised it came out all wrong. We talked for a long time, and then she asked me to go and get her some headache tablets, and well the rest you know.'

There's a moment of awkward silence. I'm not sure why Karen is telling me this. And then I understand. She wants me to know it wasn't her fault. That her daughter didn't die hating her. I am glad they made their peace.

'I'm glad you two talked,' I say. 'That would have meant a lot to her.'

'Thank you,' says Karen again. She looks like she is going to say something else but stops. 'Well I best go speak to everyone.'

* * *

I lay in bed. Kev is asleep beside me. It's been a long, rough day and I am so tired, but I can't let myself sleep. I can't have that dream again. I try to fight it, but at some point I lose. I don't notice myself falling asleep, until I wake with a jump. There's someone stood at the end of the bed looking down at us. Except someone isn't the right word, it's more a shadow, an outline.

'Kev,' I whisper. No response.

Shaking him, I am more urgent. He needs to see this. 'Kev, wake up, there's something here.'

'Hmmm,' he mutters, more asleep than awake.

'There's something here, at the end of the bed, watching us,' I whisper, never taking my eyes off the shadow.

He sits up quickly, alert now. As he does, the shadow vanishes.

He sighs 'There's nothing there Kayleigh, go back to sleep.'

'There was,' I insist, 'it disappeared as you sat up.'

'That's it,' Kev shouts. 'Enough with the crazy talk. What the Hell is wrong with you?'

I am shocked at his out-burst; I wish I could make him understand that something isn't right here. He sighs, rubbing his face and leans back against the headboard.

'I wish I knew,' I respond, quietly, staring straight ahead.

'Whatever it is, you need to snap the fuck out of it,' he snarls.

My head spins to look at him. I feel myself welling up. I understand why he's angry, it does sound crazy. The venom in his voice scares me a little though, it is so unlike him. As a tear slips down my face, his taut body slumps.

'I'm so sorry, Kayleigh. I don't know what came over me. Forgive me?'

'Of course,' I say, relieved he's his normal self again. I'm shocked to see tears in his eyes. I melt. I can't believe I was scared of him. He's hurting and I'm not helping. I think maybe I am crazy.

No, I remind myself, the priest knows something.

I can't think about that now. Now I just want everything to be ok between me and Kev. I want to be strong for him.

Kev puts his hand on my arm, gently pulling me towards him, and I relax against him, blocking out the thoughts of ghosts and demons and Ouija boards. I gently stroke his chest.

'I feel so angry sometimes,' he says 'I don't know why, or where it comes from. It's like one minute I'm fine, and then something snaps inside me. I'm probably just tired.'

'After tonight, I'll go home for a few nights,' I say. After Zach and Emma died, I've practically lived here. I can't bear the thought of not being with him, but he's right. My nightmares keep him awake and it's not fair to him. 'Let you get some sleep.'

'Is that really what you want?' he asks me.

I shake my head. It's not, I can't lie to him about that.

'Don't go,' he says, holding me tighter. 'I need you here with me. Please. I know it's not fair when I snap at you, but just please don't go'

'Ok,' I agree, relieved. I guess we are both more upset than we are letting on and neither of us is quite ready to let it go yet.

I pull away from his embrace slightly and look up at him, a sudden rush of emotion and desire sweeping me. Maybe he can read it in my face, because he leans down to me and kisses me. I kiss him back and it's like all the tension of the last few weeks needs to be released and now.

We kiss hungrily, grabbing at each other, pressing so close together we are practically one.

He pushes me onto my back, pressing on top of me, his weight making me feel safe, loved. I am so ready for this.

He pushes inside me in one hard thrust. I wrap my legs tightly around him as he thrusts hard and fast, relentlessly into me. My hips meet his thrusts eagerly, I need this.

I feel my climax building, and its there, hot and all consuming. As I cum, I feel all the tension leaving my body and I feel free in that moment. Kev isn't far behind me, and he cums hard, his face contorted, a low moan escaping his lips.

He relaxes on top of me, his breath coming in ragged pants, and I never want to let go.

Pulling out of me, he rolls onto his side and I turn to face him. He strokes me face, and kisses me.

'That's what we needed,' he says.

I nod. We did. We haven't had sex since that day, it felt wrong somehow after all what happened. I feel like I should feel guilty now, but I don't. I feel sated, and relaxed for the first time in a long time. And it feels right, not wrong.

'Yeah,' I agree. I grin and he grins back. It feels good. Maybe everything will go back to normal now. Now we have finally said goodbye, we can move on and stop living in limbo. Maybe all the crazy stuff will stop, or at least I will be able to deal with it better.

I feel my eyes closing. 'I love you,' I say.

'I love you too,' says Kev, brushing my forehead with his lips. I nod, barely registering his words as sleep claims me. For the first time in weeks, there are no nightmares.

Chapter Six

'I have to pop home for a couple of hours,' I tell Kev over a full English breakfast when he asks me what I want to do today. 'You should spend a little time with your mum.'

I feel so guilty lying to him, but if I told him the truth, we would only end up arguing, and after last night, that's the last thing I want. I feel like everything is good between us and I don't want to ruin it. Plus, he really should spend some time with his mum. No one is sure exactly when the cancer will take her, but the doctors think it will be soon.

'Is this because of last night?' he asks quietly, a hurt look passing across his face.

That look almost makes me change my mind and just stay and hold him, but I can't. I know I can't. I have to remind myself that I'm doing this for him, for us.

'No! I just need to check in that's all. Mum and dad will be worried and I just want to put their mind at rest. I promise I'll be back.'

'Ok,' he agrees, looking relieved. 'Do you want me to drop you off?'

'No,' I say, 'the walk will do me good. Burn some of this breakfast off'

Reaching across the table, he gives my hand a squeeze. 'You look fine to me.'

He winks, and I smile, feeling the butterflies in my stomach again. He looks so good, his hair still wet from the shower. Now I find myself wanting to stay for a different reason. To distract myself from this train of thought, I stand and pour us both some fresh coffee.

We finish up breakfast and I leave, kissing him goodbye.

'Say hi to your mum and dad for me,' smiles Kev.

'I will,' I reply, another pang of guilt hitting me.

I set off towards my house, the opposite direction to the church, but he stands on the doorstep watching me. I wonder if he suspects. No he can't possibly suspect; it sounds crazy even to me that I am doing this. He's just being nice, seeing me off.

I reach the end of the street and double back on myself down the next street. I am so nervous I hardly notice the chill of the breeze, hardly hear the leaves rustling on the tree lined streets.

It's only a fifteen-minute walk to the church, but by the time I get there, I feel breathless.

I try to convince myself I need to join the gym, but I know it's nothing to do with that. It's the thought of what I may be about to hear.

I push open the door and go in. The church is quiet, deserted. I hadn't banked on that, I figured Father Michaels would be here, or at least someone who would know where to find him. While I decide how to go about finding him, I walk to the front of the church and light a candle each for Zach and Emma. I'm not sure it'll help them any, but it's a nice thing to do.

As I light it, a side door I hadn't noticed opens and a man walks out. It's him. He seems to see me at the same moment I see him.

'Father,' I say realising I have no idea how to say what I came to say.

'Kayleigh, right?' he says.

I nod, muted, looking at my feet.

'I had a feeling you would be back.'

My head shoots up. 'Really?' I almost demand. He nods, unfazed by my abrupt tone.

'How can I help you?'

'I don't know where to start,' I admit.

He points to a pew. 'Come. Let's sit.'

I sit stiffly on the pew he indicates and he sits beside me. I try to compose my thoughts, and decide on the direct approach.

'Why did you keep looking at my friend's coffins yesterday?' I say.

'Ah, Kayleigh, we shouldn't talk of such things,' he says.

'Please, I need to know,' I speak too loudly and my voice echoes around the empty church. '

'Please,' I repeat, quieter now.

'You and I both know there was something other your friends in those coffins yesterday.' He looks around him. 'This is unofficial. You mustn't tell anyone about this conversation.'

I nod agreement, and he continues.

'I don't know what it was, but it was something ungodly.'

Something in the way he says the first part makes me think he's not being entirely truthful. I think he knows exactly what it was but I don't push it. I don't want him to clam up altogether.

I don't know if I'm more scared or more relieved at his words. It's good to know I'm not crazy, but as he continues, I think maybe crazy would be better.

'Your other friend, the one who spoke, you saw his eyes change didn't you?' he asks.

'You saw it too,' I breathe.

'I don't know what those three did to bring themselves to its attention child, but it means business.'

'Us four,' I blurt.

'What?'

'You said those three. There was the four of us. We did a Ouija board. A spirit came through and gave us messages. They seemed like nice messages at the time, but now I'm not so sure. They…'

He cuts me off. 'Enough. Why do you young people think it is ok to dabble in these things?'

'It was just a game,' I mutter.

'A game!' he is incredulous. 'Are you having fun?'

'No! I didn't know this would happen, please, you have to help me. I can't talk to anyone about this except Kev and he thinks I'm crazy and now it's in him isn't it. I don't know what to do!'

I burst into hysterical tears. He lets me cry until I get control over myself and hands me a tissue. I accept it gratefully, wiping my eyes and my nose.

'I'm sorry, I shouldn't have been so hard on you.'

'Please Father, what do we do next?'

'I'm afraid there is no we child,' he tells me gently. 'The catholic church no longer carries out exorcisms. It's not good for our image.'

I feel the blood rising to my cheeks. 'Not good for your image!' I splutter angrily. 'Not good for your image. My two best friends are dead, my boyfriend is next and then me, and you won't help me because you are worried how it will look?' I stand up.

'Kayleigh,' he says, calmly. He is so calm and it's making me madder. 'There's nothing I can do. I shouldn't have said anything, but I wanted you to know what you are up against. There is hope if you will just let God into your heart and have faith.'

'Faith?' I laugh. 'God? You, a representative of God just told me I'm on my own, and now you expect me to have faith? Wow, just wow.'

'I'm sorry, there is nothing more I can do.' He stands to leave, and something in his tone, his posture, tells me he is lying.

'Father, you are lying to me, please tell me what is really going on here.'

'I can't, I've said too much already. I'm sorry.'

'Please, Father, I beg you. Just tell me what you know. At least give us a fighting chance against this thing.'

Sitting back down, he puts his head in his hands. I stand, waiting. Just when I decide that's it and turn to leave, he looks up at me, his face set. 'Come into the confessional,' he says. 'It's the only place I can be sure no one is listening in.'

We make our way to the booths, him entering one side, me the other. I sit on the stool, and jump when the grate slides open.

'You must tell no one of this conversation. Promise me.'

'I promise,' I say. Who would I tell? It's hardly polite dinner party conversation is it. A bitter laugh rises in my throat and I push it back down. This priest is the only person who could believe me, who doesn't think I'm crazy. Hysterical laughter would not help.

'That spirit that was in those coffins is a demon, Kayleigh. The most powerful demon to walk amongst men. Its evil knows no bounds. It takes normal, innocent people, and grants them their heart's desire. It takes over them and kills most of them, but some, it saves. It saves them to live in. It prays on the weak, but worse it prays on the strong, corrupting them and bending them to its will.

'Once it is in someone, it leaves when it wants to, and it would take a powerful man or woman to get it out sooner. Do you understand what I am telling you?'

'Yes,' I say and I'm surprised at how calm my voice sounds. I am also surprised at how easily I am buying this. It sounds ridiculous, but how can you argue with something when you have seen the evidence?

'Are you telling me you are that man Father?'

'No.'

'I don't understand Father. How are you not that man? You know this thing. You are that man Father; you have to be. You are my only hope.' I feel tears rising again as I try desperately to understand, to persuade the priest to help me.

'I am not that man. Priests more powerful than me have tried over the years and all of them have been defeated. All of them were dead within the hour. I have no fear of dying for my God, but it would do you no good. You still wouldn't be rid of it. Something has drawn this demon to you four in particular. Something more than the Ouija board. There is a reason it chose you four, people dabble in the occult every day and don't encounter anything as evil as this. It has a purpose Kayleigh, a purpose you and your friends are somehow involved in and I can't beat that.'

Suddenly, a memory hits me. The horror of the memory brings out the tears I have been trying so desperately to hold back. Silently, they spill down my face, dripping from my chin. I make no move to wipe them away. I feel like I am locked in a paralysis brought about by my horror.

'Oh God, oh God,' I repeat over and over again, rocking back and forth on the stool. It occurs to me this is blasphemous, and probably isn't doing anything to convince the priest I am worthy of his help. It's amazing the clarity you get when everything else breaks. And that's how I feel in that moment. Broken. Defeated.

'What it is child?' His tone is gentle, almost as if he were really speaking to a child. Under any other circumstances, I would find this hugely insulting, but here, now, it makes me feel safe. Taking a deep breath, I find my voice again and it comes out in a rush.

'Father, the night we did the Ouija board, I did something. Something I shouldn't have. I didn't know it was wrong, until after wards, when Zach told me. This is all my fault. I invited it in. That's why it chose us.'

'What did you do?'

'I...' I hesitate. I can't speak. I can't tell him what I have done. How could I have been so stupid?

'Kayleigh?' he prompts gently.

'I said its name. I called it by name. Zach, Emma, Kev, it's all my fault. Oh God, what have I done? Please help me Father, please. I am begging you.' I am crying so hard now my words are unintelligible. I know I have to get control of myself. How can I expect Father Michaels to take me seriously when I am acting like this?

'Calm down Kayleigh, you are safe here.' And somehow, with his words I know that I am, that I will be. He will help me. He has to.

Calmer now, I start again.

'When we did the Ouija board, I called the spirit by name. After we were done, Zach told me it gives the spirits power and that I shouldn't have done it. I didn't know that. I unwittingly invited it in. That's its purpose with us Father, that's why it chose us. Because of me.'

'It's not your fault Kayleigh. That demon had marked your group long before you did that Ouija board. That was just the toll it used to send you it's sick messages.

'People believe that to speak a demon's name gives it power. It is the opposite, to know a demon's name gives us the power. If we know what we are dealing with, we have a fighting chance, without it we are powerless to defeat it. You saw the strength of its power that it can come into a holy place, desecrate a holy place with its vile presence and take a man before my very eyes.'

I notice he has starting using we instead of you. That's a good sign, he is coming around to helping us. I interrupt him, I can't help it.

'So we can beat it then? We can use its name against it?'

Father Michaels sits up straighter behind the grille. 'What is its name Kayleigh?'

'Its name is Scurra.'

He slumps back down, his squared shoulders becoming rounder, defeat written all over him and I feel my hopes sink.

'As I thought, it was playing with you. Scurra is the Latin word for joker. That is not its real name. I'm sorry I can't help you. The best advice I can give you is to walk away. Leave this church, leave this town and never come back. Pray that it doesn't seek you.'

'I can't do that. I can't walk away from Kev.'

'I feared you would say that. Then all I can do is wish you all the luck in the world. God be with you child.'

Before I can respond, he has left the booth, leaving me sitting alone. I sit for a while, trying to get my thoughts in order. I feel strangely calm. Calmer than I have for a long time. I know what I am up against now. I know I'm not crazy. I won't let that, that thing, take anyone else from me.

I weigh up my options. I could contact a psychic. No, I scratch that idea quickly. Most of them are fake, and even if I found a genuine one, how would I convince them I wasn't nuts? I could confront Kev, try to get him to believe me and take him to a bishop. They would have to help. I would never get him to do that though. Even if Scurra hasn't got too tight of a hold over him yet, he wouldn't go along with that.

I consider following Father Michaels through the door he left by, he has to be back there somewhere. I could try and convince him to help. No, he has made it clear there's nothing he can do for me. At least not yet.

I need more information. I know what I must do. I have to get the Ouija board out again, talk to Scurra, try and somehow get something useful. Maybe then Father Michaels will help me. I haven't written him off completely just yet.

With my new found resolve, I head back to Kev's place. I need to see him while he is still him, tell him what's happening, make him see.

I am hoping he will be a little easier to convince now I have the word of a priest that this is happening. I know I promised Father Michaels I wouldn't speak of our conversation, but I am assuming he meant anyone within the church. Or at least that's how I am justifying betraying his confidence. It's not like I'm telling anyone and everyone. Kev is involved in this, and he has a right to know what is in him. He needs to know so he can fight it.

Kev has to know what is going on. How can I not tell him?'

I walked back to Kev's with a sense of dread, almost finality hanging over me. I walked slower than I did on the way to the church yet I seem to get there faster.

My head is spinning with thoughts and ideas. I decide to tackle the problem that isn't dangerous first. It isn't dangerous, but I'm still not sure how to make it work. Getting Zach's Ouija board. Do I just turn up at his door and ask for access to his things? Maybe I should just go buy a Ouija board? Or does it have to be the same one? There is still so much I just don't know!

Trying to push these thoughts from my mind, I push open Kev's door, forcing a care free smile onto my face. At least I hope it looks care free. I find him sitting on his sofa where I left him.

'Where have you been?' he asks.

'Home,' I respond. 'I told you where I was going. Did you talk to your mum?' I try desperately to move the conversation along, I hate lying to him, but I need to gauge his mood before I plunge into my story.

'Liar,' he says, his voice dangerously calm. In my confused state, I totally missed the warning signs. The blank, expressionless face. The quiet calmness. I try to back track.

'I…I' I stutter helplessly. Get a grip Kayleigh I tell myself. 'I popped to the shops.' It sounds like a lie, even to me.

'Lies!' He is yelling now, the anger from last night clouding his face. He slams his fist on the arm of the sofa, sending a small cloud of dust spinning through the sunlight streaming in the window. 'You are a liar Kayleigh. I don't like being lied to.'

I back up a step, uncertain what to do. I want to run but I can't. I have to reach Kev. He is still in there.

'Kev, please,' I say, hating the way my voice sounds so shaky, so weak, like I am already beaten. 'Don't be like this.'

His face changes. The angry expression disappears and his posture becomes more natural, more like him.

'What's really going on here? Is there something I should know?' he asks, his voice back to normal. The anger has gone, but it has been replaced with something that breaks my heart a little. Fear.

He sounds so sad, so worried. I decide on the spur of the moment to tell him the truth now. It seems like a good time. He is him again, and he seems open to knowing what's going on. It might be my best chance. I take a deep breath.

'Don't be mad,' I say. 'I went to see Father Michaels. Kev, when we did that Ouija board, we didn't talk to any ordinary spirit. It was a demon. We have to find a way to get rid of it. It killed Zach and Emma and now it's got a hold on you. I can't lose you. I can't.'

I can feel myself getting hysterical, my words tumbling out. It does sound crazy, even to me. I take a few deep breaths, willing him to believe me.

'This again,' he breathes. 'Kayleigh, you need help.'

'You're right, I do. Just not the help you mean. I need help getting this, this Thing out of you and out of our lives for good.'

I touch his arm.

'You know me Kev. You know I'm not crazy. I don't believe in any of this stuff, but that doesn't matter anymore. I have to believe in it now because this is happening whether you like it or not. I love you, please, let me help you,' I finish.

He springs off the sofa so fast it flies backwards a couple of feet. I jump back. He walks towards me with an eerie grace, almost cat like. I've never seen him like this. He is angry and calm at the same time. Dangerous. Sexy.

I back up until I am against the wall with nowhere else to go. He stalks toward me until we are mere inches apart. This isn't Kev, this is Scurra. How did I not see this before?

He is clever. He acted hurt to get the truth from me and I fell for it. I am angry with myself, but right now, I am more scared. I am scared of what he will do to me, to himself, but more than that, I am scared that I kind of like this new Kev. Unpredictable, edgy, and somehow, so hot. Maybe he is right. Maybe I do need help. I can't think about that now.

I have to get my Kev back out somehow.

'Kev I know you're in there. Fight it!' I say, trying to keep the tremor out of my voice. 'Come on, fight.' My voice sounds stronger than I feel.

'You would do anything for me?' he asks quietly, gently brushing a piece of hair out of my face.

I nod mutely. Did it work? Did he fight it off?

'Anything?'

'Of course.'

'Then fuck me,' he says, his tone never changing. 'Fuck me now on this floor like the dirty little whore that you are.'

I feel my eyes fill with tears. This isn't Kev. My minding is whirling again. I have to buy some time, a way to get out of here. A part of me wants this. A tiny, self-destructive part. The part that is too tired to fight it, that wants to just curl up in a ball and pretend it isn't happening, that it's just a fight and we will be laughing about it by this tomorrow. I can't give in to this part. I know I can't.

I force a laugh. It sounds shaky, even to me. 'Not here,' I say. 'Let's go to bed.'

I go to walk past him, but he grabs me roughly by the shoulders, pinning me in place. His face is inches from mine. I recognise every part of it. His mouth, his nose, his beautiful eyes. Except now, his eyes have a yellow tinge, and his mouth is twisted with rage.

'Let's get one thing clear here, Kayleigh,' he says, the contempt dripping from every word. 'I call the shots. 'We do this here and now or you walk away and never come back.'

'Then I'll walk away.' I raise my chin defiantly. 'You are not Kev. You are a monster.'

He takes a step back, releasing my wrists. I step around him. If I can just get away from him, I'll find a way to get that Ouija board and help him. I am half way towards the door, to freedom, when I hear a movement. I glance back and he covers the distance between us in two easy strides. I try to run, but I am too late. He grabs me and throws me backwards to the floor like I am a rag doll. Pain explodes through my head as it hits the tiles. Ignoring it as best I can, I try to roll over, to crawl away, but he's on me.

Grabbing me, he forces me to turn over so I am on my back looking up at him. He is still angry, but worse, I see something new. Hatred, contempt. It's like he sees my weakness.

I am terrified. I can't move, can't think, but I know I have to get away somehow. I can't let this happen.

He grabs my legs, forcing them apart and kneeling between them. I hit out blindly, and I feel one of my fists connect with his chest. It's like he doesn't feel it.

I keep hitting out with both hands. Swatting them away angrily, he makes a grab for my wrists. He crouches over me, holding my wrists flat to the floor with one of his hands. The other hand drags my top up and bra up, exposing my breasts. He lightly trails a finger over my nipples, almost lazily.

'Stupid girl,' he hisses. 'Did you really think I would let you leave? I gave you a chance to do this the easy way and you chose him over me. I am powerful, more powerful than you can possibly know. He is weak. He let me in. Now you will do the same, but in a very different way.'

I know what's about to happen. I can't let it go any further. I have to fight him off, get away. I can't think, can barely breathe. In a blind panic I writhe and twist, trying to throw him off. My legs kick at his back, but it's useless. He's so strong, it's like I'm not even there.

His hand leaves my nipples and hitches my skirt up, forcing my bum off the floor long enough to drag it around my hips. He rips my panties off and one in fluid thrust he's inside me.

'No!' I shout. 'No, no! Kev, no, get off me!'

'Let me make this clear,' he snarls. 'I. Am. Not. Fucking. Kevin.' Each word drips with hatred. On the last word, he slaps me hard across my cheek with his free hand. My head flies to the side, blood pouring from my lip. Momentarily stunned, I lay panting.

He thrusts hard, filling me, stretching me. He feels huge, and with mounting horror, I realise that part of me is enjoying the sensation. The tingling feeling brings me back to my sense. No! I won't give in to this.

I continue trying to throw him off, trying to work my hands free. As I struggle, my movement, the fight seems to spur him on. He thrusts into me over and over. I go limp again. I can't fight him off. Tears run down my face and I whisper 'No' over and over again to no avail.

His thrusts are getting faster, harder. It will be over soon. He's close. I close my eyes, trying to think of something, anything except what is happening.

As his immense cock repeatedly bangs into me, I feel my body responding. My hips meet his thrusts. He lets my hands go, confident he has me in his power.

This is my chance, I should claw his eyes out, do whatever is necessary to get away from him, but I don't.

Instead, I rake my nails down his back. It is no longer about fighting him off. It is a response to the overwhelming desire building inside me. He stops thrusting and instead of relief, I feel unsated, I need to feel him move inside me, to climax. My hips continue to thrust, needing to feel him inside me.

'Look at me,' he pants, the hatred gone from his voice, replaced with lust. It turns me on more and eagerly, I open my eyes.

'Tell me you want it, whore.'

I don't speak. I can't. I am mesmerized by his eyes; the yellow colour is appealing in a way, beautiful almost. I never noticed that before.

He moves his hips slightly, and a low moan escapes me.

'Tell me.'

I can't hold back any longer. A mass of feelings floods me. Guilt, disgust, but mostly overwhelming desire, an almost primal need. He has awakened in me feelings I didn't know I had.

'I want it,' I say breathlessly.

'Whore,' he snarls. Somehow, this only adds to the excitement.

He starts slowly, teasing me.

'Please,' I beg. I am ashamed yet unashamed at the same time. 'Please.'

He pulls back, so far he's almost out of me and then he rams in, so hard I cry out. Over and over he rams into me, hurting me, filling me, sating me.

I feel my climax coming. There is no gentle build up. It is there, dragging a scream from my lips as I cum. I have felt nothing like this. I am flying, I am on fire. Every nerve in my body is screaming. It is agony, but such sweet agony. I never want it to end. He continues thrusting and each time he does, another wave of ecstasy washes over me.

I throw my head back, feel the tendons standing out on my neck, the pleasure so intense I lose all thought, all awareness, there is only me and him in the whole world. Me and him and this burning, delicious agony.

Just when I think I can't take it anymore, I feel him go rigid. With an animal grunt he spurts his warmth inside me. Panting, he withdraws and flops on his back beside me.

As my breathing returns to normal and my heart rate slows down, the full extent of what has just happened hits me. I have been raped, violated and the worst part? I loved it.

I feel guilt, shame, like I want to shower and never stop scrubbing my skin. I also feel empty; like I will never be whole again without him inside of me. I want to run away and never see him again. I want him back inside me, now. I have never felt so conflicted.

The rational part of me, back in action now the intense pleasure is over, and I listen to it. I stand up, absent-mindedly wiping the blood away from my chin. I can taste it, coppery in my mouth. It tastes like pain, pleasure, a reminder of what I could have if I give in.

I have to get out of here. Father Michaels was right. I should never have even attempted to take this thing on alone.

I pull my clothes back to their rightful places, barely noticing the lank of panties, and as I do I notice the blood under my finger nails. I smile at the memory, then catch myself. What have I become? Am I really such a slave to my desire that one good fuck means I turn my back on everything that is right? On Kev? That does the job, and brings me back to me sense.

I walk to the door. I need to get out of here. Now. I don't think I could even try to resist him now. As my hand touches the door handle, Kev speaks from the floor where is still laying.

'Don't go,' he implores. And it is him. The venom has gone from his voice. I feel a tug of disappointment, followed by a huge rush of shame.

I turn towards him as I hear movement. He stands. Tears are running down his face. Part of me wants to hold him and tell him everything will be ok whether I believe that or not, and part of me feels disgust at his show of weakness. Scurra is strong. He knows what he wants and he takes it. My heart aches for Kev, but part of my body aches for what is inside of him

I take a moment to clear my thoughts. Thoroughly disgusted with myself for even thinking I could want that thing back in Kev, I search for what to say. I need to get away. I can't think with him so close to me.

'Kev,' I say. I don't have the words. How do I tell him I'm sorry? I feel like I cheated on him. How can I even begin to explain that I enjoyed what that thing did to me, that I can still feel myself wet between my legs, wanting more. Needing more.

'You're bleeding,' he says, gesturing towards my lip. I reach up and wipe away the last bit of blood that has trickled out. Gingerly, I touch my lip where it is cut. It doesn't feel too bad, barely a scratch, but it stings a little as I touch it, bringing another wave of desire.

What is happening to me? How have I become so easily swayed?

'Please,' he says, his voice breaking through my thoughts. 'I'm so sorry. It wasn't me, I swear it. You were right all along, I was just too scared to admit it. I thought I could fight it, hold it at bay. I wasn't strong enough and you got hurt. More than hurt. I don't know what to say, please believe me.'

I don't move, I am rooted to the spot, my head still swirling with mixed emotion, my face blank, expressionless. I am scared to speak. I am scared of what I will say.

'Say something K, please,' he begs. Again, that split response. Half of me breaking for him, half of me disgusted by him. All of me lost, confused.

'I enjoyed it,' I whisper, my expression still not changing, my body still motionless, unresponsive. I need him to know he's not the monster, I am. How could I enjoy what that thing did to me? But it's more than that. I need to hurt him like he hurt me. I need him to know what I am feeling, but I don't have the words to tell him, so instead I lash out, using the one phrase that will break him even more. Hating myself for it, but doing it all the same.

'I loved it.'

It's not even close to enough but it's all I have.

'You're not to blame. That, that thing makes you feel things, makes you do things. Things you would never do. And it makes you like them.'

He understands. He gets it, he finally gets it.

More than that, he isn't weak. My words that were said in spite to break him don't break him. They show me he is strong. Stronger than I gave him credit for.

I am the weak one. Scurra used Kev to get to me, to break me, and it is only now I am seeing it.

Only now I am seeing how close I came to breaking, how close I came to giving in.

Before I have time to think about it, I turn and throw myself into his arms, almost knocking him off his feet. He strokes my hair and whispers my name as we sob, clinging to each other. How did we get ourselves into this mess?

I calm myself down and it seems Kev has done the same. I pull back slightly and look at him. He has control of himself again. I reach my hand up and wipe away the tears. I kiss him gently on the mouth and he kisses me back. It feels sweet, innocent. Normal.

My lip stings slightly and I feel nothing, no desire. I wince a little.

'I'm sorry,' he says, gently kissing the cut. 'How can you ever forgive me?'

And now I find the words to say what I needed to say. 'I can forgive you because it wasn't you. Like it wasn't me enjoying what he did to me. It's his hold, his influence, but if we stick together, we can fight it. I know we can.'

He nods, his jaw set in steely determination. We hold each in silence a little longer.

Finally, regretfully, I step back from his embrace and take his hand.

'I have to go, but I swear I'll be back,' I say

'Where are you going?' he asks.

'It doesn't matter; you have to trust me on this.'

'I do trust you, but you need to trust me too. Don't keep me in the dark K.'

He's right. Even if he tries to stop me, I need to be honest with him. I lied about where I was going earlier today and look where that got me. The thing inside him feeds on lies, uses them to play with us and turn us against each other.

'Zach's,' I tell him. 'I have to find a way to get that Ouija board. We need to find out as much as we can about Scurra.'

'Ok,' he agrees, 'But why can't I come with you?'

'I don't think it's a good idea,' I reply. 'What if Scurra comes through and you can't control it. Imagine what it could say to Zach's mother.'

Reluctantly, he nods his agreement.

With one last kiss, I turn and leave, making my way through the garden, through the house and towards the front door.

'Kayleigh, can you come in here a minute a please, I need to talk to you.'

It's Kev's mother. Going to Zach's house is important, but Kev's mother is important too.

It can wait an hour I decide and walk to her make shift sick room.

Knocking lightly, I go in.

Sitting up in bed, Rose looks pale, paler than usual.

She points towards a sofa placed beside her bed. 'Sit down.'

I sit and she continues.

'I haven't got much longer,' she begins.

I interrupt her. 'Don't talk like that.'

'Kayleigh,' she smiles at him. 'We both know it's true. Let's not waste time debating it. I don't know how much help I can be, but let me tell you what I know about Scurra.'

Chapter 8

'How do you know about Scurra?'

How much of our conversations has she heard? No, it can't be that, I reason, we haven't said anything in ear shot of her room. How does she know his name? That I would recognise it?

My mind is reeling. How can she know about Scurra? Why didn't she tell us sooner? Does she know a way to get rid of him? There's so many questions, I hardly know where to start.

I open my mouth to blurt out more questions, but holding up a hand for silence, Rose continues. 'It's a very long story and I'm tired. Please don't interrupt, I will tell you everything, but I need to start at the beginning.'

'Ok,' I agree. I'm not sure I can keep from interrupting, but I'll try. She does look tired and I need to hear this, all of it.

Shuffling slightly to find a comfortable position, I prepare myself to hear what Rose has to say. I am not prepared in the slightest for what I am about to hear.

* * *

Rose sits back against her pillows, the exhaustion showing in her face. She looks pale against the blue of her nightie, too pale.

I feel drained emotionally and so over whelmed. My head is spinning with the enormity of what I have heard and I need time to process. Time I don't have.

I don't know what to say to Rose. I stutter and splutter, making false starts until eventually I stop even trying to speak, to get my thoughts into order.

Rose smiles weakly. 'It's a lot to take in.'

'Yes,' I agree. Finally getting myself together a bit, I continue. 'I need to go and talk to Kev. You rest and we'll be back as soon as I've filled him in on everything.'

Rose nods her agreement, her eyes already closing. As I reach the door, Rose's weak voice stops me.

'Don't let him hurt my son.'

'I won't,' I promise. And I mean it.

I re-trace my steps back to Kev's place and go in. As my hand reaches for the handle, I find myself scared it won't be Kev inside. A small part of me hopes it's not. I push that thought away, disgusted at myself as I feel a smile play over my face at the memory of what just happened. Pushing the thoughts away, I remind myself that that was Scurra playing with me, humiliating me.

'That was quick,' Kev says, looking up from the TV. With mostly relief I see it is Kev.

'I didn't go,' I say. 'I've been with your mum. We need to talk.'

He looks worried now, a frown creasing his brow. 'What is it? What happened? Is mum ok?'

'She's fine,' I reassure him 'but she has told me a lot of things. Things she hasn't told anyone before. Things I need to tell you.'

I sit down beside him and reach for his hand. And I tell him everything Rose told me.

* * *

Rose's story

9pm, it's a Saturday in July 1973. Rose couldn't remember the exact date. Normally, she was allowed to stay up late on weekends, but not tonight. Tonight, her parents were going out, and her 16-year-old cousin, Sally, had been drafted in to babysit her. Rose was kind of annoyed.

'I don't need a babysitter, I'm 12 years old,' she had announced huffily to her mother upon being informed of the night's plans.

Her mother had ignored her protests. Now she lay sulkily in bed, hearing her parents say goodbye to Sally. Hearing Sally respond. She knew how the night would go. Half an hour after her parents left, Sally's friends would arrive. Three other girls. Rose could never get their names straight, could never remember which one was which. One thing she never forget was her intense hatred for those girls.

They had it so easy. Could stay up as late as they liked and Rose guessed when their parents went out, they didn't need a babysitter.

The first time Sally babysat, Rose had been quite excited. She could be one of the girls, if only for one night. She had laid awake, listening for their arrival. Upon hearing them, she had gone downstairs, determined to prove to them she was as fun as they were, mature and ready to have a good gossip about boys and the other girls from their school. It would be so great Monday when she went to school and the popular girls from the final year of school were her friends.

It hadn't turned out as planned. They had all stopped talking when she entered the room.

'Great,' one of them remarked. 'I thought you said she would be asleep.'

'She was supposed to be,' Sally had answered, the scorn evident in her voice. 'Go back to bed Rose.'

'But I thought I could sit and chat with you all for a while,' Rose responded hopefully. 'We could be friends.'

They had laughed. 'Yeah, right,' Sally had said.

Rose felt the tears fill her eyes, and ran from the room before the girls could see she was crying. Up the stairs, slamming her door and throwing herself on the bed, she cried. She had never forgotten that moment, and often found herself planning an elaborate revenge on the girls. She would be the popular one, they would be the losers.

The door slamming shut and excited voices greeting each other startled Rose out of her thoughts.

'Tonight's the night,' she heard one of them say.

The night for what Rose wondered. Silently slipping out of bed and across her room, she eased the door open and crept onto the landing. The sitting room door was ajar and if she strained her ears, she could hear them chatting.

At first, they talked about school, boys, the usual, but Rose could sense that something was different. They seemed to be going through the motions.

As the grandfather clock in the hall struck 10, scaring Rose half to death, every girl went silent. So this is what they had been waiting for. But why? After a few minutes of silence, Rose could hear Sally talking in a very low voice. It was so quiet she could no longer make out the words. It sounded like a series of questions, but if anyone was answering them, Rose couldn't hear it.

She had to know what was going on, so she crept down the stairs, making a point of avoiding the third stair down, knowing its loud creak would give her away.

Reaching the door and peering through the crack, Rose was unsure what she was seeing. The four girls were sat around the coffee table, a board laid out in front of them. It looked like they were playing a board game of some kind, but Sally seemed to be asking the game questions.

In a low voice, Sally asked 'Scurra, are you here?'

Scurra, what did that mean? Rose had no idea, but she watched, fascinated, as the girls pushed a glass she hadn't even noticed around the table. What sort of game was this? And they thought she was stupid!

As she watched, a dark shadow formed above the table. She rubbed her eyes, she must be more tired than she wanted to admit. But no, the girls saw it too, they were looking at it with obvious glee.

'This is it,' Sally said. 'The moment we have been waiting for. Girls, prepare to have your lives changed, your biggest desires granted, and your every wish come true.'

They giggled, but to Rose it sounded like a nervous giggle.

The dark haired one, it might have been Sarah, it might have been Liz spoke up. 'Sal, is this a good idea?'

Sally turned to her, the anger flashing in her eyes. 'We have been working towards this for months. There's no going back.'

Liz nodded, but she didn't look convinced.

The black shadow seemed to be getting blacker, as if it was solidifying in front of them. Rose knew she should have been afraid, but she wasn't. As she watched, the shadow passed through each of the girls. She could only clearly see Sally's face, and as the shadow passed through her, she could swear her eyes turned briefly yellow.

What happened next seemed to happen fast and slow at the same time, Rose couldn't be sure exactly what happened, but those next few minutes changed her life forever. The girls in the room seemed as transfixed on the shadow as she was, their rapt eyes staring up at it.

Rose felt something brush her cheek, but when she turned her head slightly, there was nothing there. She heard a deep, masculine voice close to her ear, close enough she should be able to feel breath on her skin, yet there was no movement, nothing. Just the voice.

'Little Rose,' the voice said. 'You and me, we could be destined for great things. Those girls may have called me here, but they are nothing compared to you.'

Rose swallowed, not daring to answer and risk drawing attention to herself. The voice continued.

'Let me in Rose, and everything you want is yours. I will make you popular, successful. Those girls will be long gone, distant memories, and you and I will rule the world.'

It sounded good, too good to be true. Rose wondered if she was dreaming. This couldn't be real.

'You are not dreaming Rose, this is very real. You don't have much time left though before the girls realise their power, power that could be yours. All you have to do is say yes.'

'Yes,' Rose said, barely a whisper. Then louder, 'Yes!'

She felt something enter her head, a power she had never dreamed possible. She felt alive for the first time in her life. The world was hers and she was about to take it. She could feel a tingling sensation all over her body, from her head down to her littlest toe. It felt good. Really good.

Sally was on her feet and the other girls weren't far behind her.

'Get out,' she screamed at Rose.

'I think not,' replied Rose calmly. 'This is my house, you get out, all of you before I make you get out.'

It was a strange feeling, Rose knew she had spoken, yet it was like she hadn't spoken. She had made no conscious decision to speak, her mouth was working independently of her, but she liked the cold authority in her voice, liked the way all the girls looked her, fear in their eyes.

'Now!' she shouted, raising her arms as she did so. As her arms raised, the glass, long forgotten on the table broke. Broke wasn't the right word. Exploded was more the word. Shards of razor sharp glass flew through the air, cutting the girls and littering the room.

They didn't have to be asked again. They fled, leaving Rose behind. As they ran down the path, the sitting room window exploded in the same way as the glass, flying over the manicured lawn and the newly planted apple tree in the centre, hitting Sally and her cronies on their exposed arms and faces.

And Rose laughed. Oh how she laughed.

'Rose! Are you alright?' Her mother's arms encircled her protectively. 'I'm so sorry, I should never have left you with those girls.'

Rose allowed herself to be held for a minute, then she slowly uncurled from the ball she was sitting in in the corner of Mrs Lane's sitting room.

'It's ok mum, it's not your fault,' she said, tears running down her cheeks. Allowing herself to be hugged once more, no one saw the smile that played over her lips.

Scurra had told her exactly what to do, and willingly, she had followed his instructions to the letter. First, she had destroyed the game the girls had been playing, taking it into the back yard and holding a match to it, watching the ashes blow away on the wind. Scurra told her it was called a Ouija board, and the girls had used it to summon him, to grant their wishes, but Scurra had wanted to be friends with Rose, not them.

Next, he told her to bolt out of the front door in her nightdress, and bare feet, screaming and scared. Her feet would be cut, but she would have to live with that if she wanted him to be able to stay. She was to run across the road and knock on Mrs Lane's door, and tell her what had happened. Or at least their version of what had happened.

So she had. Dishevelled and bleeding, crying, she had knocked on Mrs Lane's door. Mrs Lane had pulled her inside, leading her into the sitting room, her feet leaving a bloody pattern on the carpet.

'What happened,' she demanded to know.

'I, I'm not sure,' Rose had stammered. 'My cousin and her friends were babysitting me. I was asleep upstairs and I was woken by a loud noise. I got out of bed, and opened my door, started to go downstairs. Sally, that's my cousin, she was there, a chunk of broken glass in her hand. She was threatening the other girls with it. They managed to get past her and ran for the door. Sally ran back into the sitting room and threw something through the window, the glass exploded over them as they ran, and Sally chased after them. I was just glad she didn't see me.'

'Dear Lord,' Mrs Lane had cried, and Rose had to try really hard not sneer. 'Are you hurt? What time are your parents due back? We need to call the police.'

She was panicking, just had Scurra had said she would.

Rose was calm, but she had to act as though she too was in panic.

'Just my feet,' she said. 'I don't know when my parents are due back. I want my mum' She had turned up the crying a notch. Not enough to appear hysterical, just enough to appear scared and vulnerable.

The rest of the time had passed in a blur. Mrs Lane had wrapped her in a blanket, and bandaged her feet, removing a large chunk of glass from one of them. She had sent her husband to the police station. When she had finished bandaging her feet, Rose had made her way to the far corner and huddled in the blanket, ignoring Mrs Lane's pleas for her to sit on the couch, refusing to answer any questions. Rocking gently back and forth.

A frantic Mrs Lane had alternated between trying to coax her to drink some sweet tea and watching out of the window for her parents to arrive home. When their car finally pulled up, Rose heard her father's angry voice shouting about the broken window, her mother calling her name, and Mrs Lane telling them where she was.

Then she was in her mother's arms, Mrs Lane was telling her father what had happened, and Mr Lane was arriving back, a policeman in tow.

Rose's mother had refused to have her answer any questions right away.

'She has been through enough tonight Officer,' she had said firmly. 'I suggest you find those girls and question them.'

Rose had been carried back home by her father and placed back in bed, her mother issuing a sedative.

The next morning, Rose awoke, and went down to join her parents for breakfast. As she neared the top of the stairs, she heard her father's voice 'Thank you Officer,' followed by the front door closing. She could hear her mother crying in the kitchen.

Her father spotted her standing at the top of the stairs, and beckoned her down, leading her to the kitchen too.

'What happened?' she asked groggily, still feeling the after effects of the sedative.

Her mother and father exchanged looks as Rose reached for the cereal and poured herself a bowl, adding a spoonful of sugar and covering them with milk.

'She might as well hear it from us,' her mother said, wiping at her eyes with a tissue.

Nodding, her father looked at her. 'The police found Sally and her friends at one of their houses,' he began. 'The three girls had their throats cut, and Sally's wrists were cut. They found a note explaining she was sorry, she didn't know what had come over her. The police say she murdered her friends then killed herself.'

Rose paused, her loaded spoon part way to her mouth. She wasn't sure how she felt about this. She had wanted revenge, wanted those girls out of her way, but like this? It was too much, too drastic.

The spoon fell to the floor and Rose began to cry. 'I'm sorry,' she repeated over and over again, 'it wasn't meant to be like this.'

'It's ok,' her mother soothed, holding her, stroking her hair. 'It's not your fault honey, none of us saw this coming. Ssshhh.'

Rose knew it was her fault, all her fault, but what could she do? She could hardly admit it could she. And if she was totally honest with herself, a large part of her was pretty pleased with how things turned out.

* * *

Eight weeks on and Rose was finding it hard to decide whether she was happy about Scurra being with her or not. She couldn't think properly; he knew her every thought. One thing she did know is she was happy with the new found popularity. Everyone wanted to be her friend. She was kind of a bitch at times, but it didn't matter, she was the popular one now. No one would call her out on her behaviour because no one wanted to risk being excluded. Scurra certainly delivered on his promise. He could grant her her every wish.

It was getting harder and harder to control him though. At first, it was easy. If she called to him, he came. She could feel him inside her the whole time, but she was the one running the show. Or so she had thought. She wondered now if that had ever been true. Now she didn't have to call him, he was in charge. She got a bit of time where she could say what she chose, act how she chose but it was getting less and less often. She spent most of the time she was in control crying and apologising to her parents for the appalling way she had behaved. They forgave her, they blamed the grief they felt they had caused, but that made her feel even more guilty.

She no longer even tried to resist Scurra – what was the point? She was a weakling, a child, and he was an all-powerful Demon, something he never let her forget. It wasn't all bad though. He did grant her whatever she wanted, it was the way he went about it she had the problem with.

After his latest outburst, his way of getting her curfew extended (she actually had a social life since he made her popular), which involved much shouting and cursing, followed by eerie calmness, she had seen fear in her Mother's eyes. Her Mother had agreed to the curfew because she was afraid to do anything else.

In that moment, Rose would have given anything to have rid of Scurra and go back to being her unpopular, normal self. That was the one desire Scurra would never grant. He was here to stay. He had made it clear that if she told her parents what was happening, there would be consequences.

He showed her visions of herself locked away in an institution, a metal clamp holding her head in place as her brain was repeatedly blasted with electricity. She was too scared to test him on it – she had seen him in action and she knew he was capable of that and much worse.

Exactly one month ago today, sitting in her room, a forgotten book open in her lap, she heard her parents talking downstairs. Either Scurra made her hearing better, or her parents were that stressed out, they were shouting. Whatever the reason, she could hear them clear as day.

'I don't know how much more of this I can take,' her mother had said, the tears evident in her voice.

'I know,' responded her father, 'but what can we do? She is just a child, a grief stricken child.'

'That thing is not my daughter, her mother responded, her voice getting louder, stronger, all evidence of tears gone as her voice hardened.

'Now come on dear, don't talk like that. Remember what Dr. Jessop said.'

Dr Jessop, their GP had been called in to see Rose when the mood swings started. He informed her parents this was an effect of what happened the night Sally babysat and that it would just take time.

'Dr Jessop said she would have mood swings. These are not mood swings, it's like her whole personality has changed.'

Her parents went back and forth on whether or not she was getting worse. Of course she was, Rose herself knew she was. Scurra was clever though. He kept the worst of it for times when she was alone with her mother. It explained some of the glances her father gave her mother when he thought Rose wasn't looking.

Eventually, her father conceded that Rose should be sent to see a psychiatrist, if nothing else, it would convince his wife her reaction to grief was normal. And when it was proved to be normal, maybe his wife would consider seeing the psychiatrist too, this whole incident had obviously taken its toll on her too. Why else would she insist Rose wasn't Rose anymore?

Rose had expected Scurra to be on his best behaviour for the psychiatrist. He would act like a perfectly well behaved 12-year-old girl and there would be no doubt her mother was mentally unstable and Rose herself was fine.

Scurra had other ideas. On the way to the first appointment, he let Rose know he would be terrifying the psychiatrist to a point where they would never have to return. Rose's head was his, not some quack's.

Rose was actually pretty relieved to hear this. She would never be able to lie convincingly to a psychiatrist!

True to his word, Scurra put on quite a show at the first session. He spoke through Rose in a deep, masculine voice. He told the psychiatrist he was a Demon who lived inside Rose and that she was his. He told him they would not be returning, and that if the psychiatrist knew what was good for him, he would be writing Rose up as cured. He also gave him a very detailed description of what actually happening the night Sally and her friends died. He went on to say that it would be a real shame if anything like that happened to the psychiatrist's wife and children.

Twenty minutes into that first session, the terrified psychiatrist called in Rose's parents and demanded they take her away. When questioned, he told her parents he believed her to be possessed and that it was a priest they needed, not a psychiatrist.

Feeling vindicated, Rose's mother had turned on her father, berating him for not believing her sooner. Still a little sceptical, her father had no real argument. The psychiatrist he had insisted was the best in the business had confirmed his wife's fears. Maybe it was true and he was a terrible father for not seeing it sooner.

With nowhere left to turn, her distraught parents took the psychiatrist's advice and called in their local priest. After a brief consultation, he agreed with the psychiatrist's evaluation and the exorcism was duly scheduled.

Chapter 9

'Stop,' said Kev.

I stopped talking and looked at him questioningly. 'I just need a minute,' he said.

White faced and shaking, Kev stands up, crossing to the kitchenette and getting himself a glass of water. Taking a couple of small sips, he seems to get control of himself. The shaking has stopped, although he is still a little pale, the strain clear on his face.

I feel so bad being the one to tell him this about his mother, but I couldn't let Rose go through re-telling the story, and he has to know what had happened.

'Oh my God,' he breathed. 'What happened? Why didn't the priest get rid of it? How has it come back? Why would it let the psychiatrist know it was there?'

'Your mum said the demon was clever, much cleverer than she gave him credit for. She was still looking at this through the eyes of a naïve little girl. He knew that the only way he could stay without fighting her every step of the way was for her to give him permission to stay. He engineered the whole exorcism to make that happen.'

He comes back, sitting back down beside me. 'Carry on, I need to hear how this thing ends.'

Taking a deep breath, I began talking again.

Rose's Story – Part 2

The day of the exorcism rolled around. It started out much like any other, until that fateful knock at the door.

Rose heard Father O'Malley pass some pleasantries with her parents, then she heard the three of them come up the stairs.

The bedroom door opened and Father O'Malley stepped in followed by her parents.

'Hello Rose,' said Father O'Malley.

'Good evening Father,' she responded.

'Rose....' he began. She didn't hear the rest. Scurra forced her back and took over. His power seemed to be growing. He took over her whole mind, stopping her from seeing or hearing what was going on in the room.

She heard only him, and then only the parts he spoke directly to her. He told her he was scared to leave the Earth, scared to go on to the afterlife. He apologised for his behaviour, saying he had gone too far, promising to behave better if she would only let him stay.

In that moment, to Rose, he sounded like a scared child and she reluctantly agreed to let him stay. She promised to let the priest think he had won, and in turn, Scurra promised to lay low for a while, and allow her to re-connect with her parents.

Suddenly, Rose is back in control. For a fleeting second, she thinks Scurra is gone and she panics. She feels the colour drain from her face, feels sweat beading on her skin.

From the corner of the room, her mother throws herself on Rose, hugging and kissing her. Suddenly, Rose feels Scurra's presence deep in her mind, and crying with relief, she knows she can never let him go. She won't return to life as a nobody.

55

She knows she has to convince Father O'Malley and her parents that it is over.

'Thank you Father,' she says quietly to Father O'Malley.

'You are welcome my child,' he responds.

Rose breathes a silent sigh of relief. He believes her. They pulled it off! Her and Scurra truly are going to rule the world.

* * *

'That's it,' I say, relieved it's all out in the open now. 'Your mum was tired and I knew I needed to come and tell you what was going on.'

I'm not sure how Kev will react. He surprises me by saying exactly what I was thinking. I thought I would have to push to get him to agree to this and I am further relieved that I won't have to.

'We need to go and talk to my mum.' It's not a request, it's a statement. I didn't realise how much I was dreading the argument I thought we would have until it doesn't come. I feel like the world has just been lifted off my shoulders.

He stands and I stand with him. We walk to the house, to Rose's room, and he knocks on her door.

'Come in,' she responds, and I'm pleased to hear her voice is a little stronger. She has rested while I was gone and sounds more like herself.

Taking my hand, Kev pushes open the door and we go in.

He crosses the room to his mother, kisses her cheek and sits down, pulling me down next to him, his hand still holding mine.

'Mum,' he starts and falters.

'It's ok,' she says, 'I've been so scared of you finding out about this, so ashamed of what I am, what I allowed myself to become. I could never tell anyone about this, but now I know I have to, I'm glad to finally share it with someone. I'm just sorry that burden has fallen to you. I know it's a lot to ask of you already, but I have one more thing I must ask of you. Please don't tell your father about this. I couldn't bear him thinking I was forced to be with him. I love him and that's one thing that is all me.'

'Of course I won't tell him mum, but I know he wouldn't think any less of you. I certainly don't.'

'Thank you,' she says quietly, the tears standing out in her eyes making them glisten.

'There's still somethings I don't understand though. Why didn't the priest know he was still in there and why did Scurra reveal himself to the psychiatrist? Wouldn't it have been easier to just fake normality?'

'I'm not sure what happened with the priest. Maybe he did know deep down, but it was easier to think this would be a happy ever after moment. Or maybe he was afraid.'

Kev nods, seemingly satisfied with that explanation. 'And the psychiatrist?'

'Scurra was clever that day – he got me to agree to letting him stay. He also made a big mistake. He let me know he had a weakness. He had to be invited to stay. I didn't know if I could use that in any way, but it was sure good to know he wasn't as all powerful as I had first feared. If only I had been strong enough to let him go, if only I had cared less about popularity.'

'It's not easy to not care what people think when you are so young.' I said. Partly to make her feel better, but partly because it was true. I had seen first-hand how cruel girls at school could be to anyone they deemed to be less popular than them.

Rose threw me a grateful smile and continued.

'Over the coming years, Scurra laid pretty low. He used charm to get me what I wanted rather than fear and I was truly happy. I even started to think maybe I had misjudged Scurra. Maybe the things I had perceived as nasty where just a necessary evil. Maybe he wasn't so bad after all. I was soon brought back to earth with a bang.

'On my eighteenth birthday, my parents sat me down and asked how much I remembered from the night of the exorcism. Only, they didn't use the word exorcism, they asked me what I remembered of Father O'Malley's visit when I was sick.

'I answered honestly that the exorcism was mostly a blur. They seemed surprised that I had known it was an exorcism, but they tried to hide their surprise. Mum told me she believed that Father O'Malley took the demon into him because he died shortly after completing the exorcism.

'That's when I knew. Scurra hadn't changed at all. He killed Father O'Malley. As mum was telling me what she believed happened, Scurra spoke to me in my mind. He claimed it was because the priest was suspicious. I knew it was more than that. Father O'Malley wasn't stupid; he wouldn't have told anyone his suspicions even if he had them until they had been confirmed. I knew it and I was sure Scurra knew it too. He was getting darker and I didn't like it. I was no longer a child and I took control. I fought him down and I refused to let him take me over any more.

'I have fought him for years, and I am tired of it. I even moved to another country to try and out run him. That sounds so stupid now, but it seemed like a good idea at the time.'

I nod, encouraging her to go on. It doesn't sound that stupid. Father Michaels gave me the same advice at one time, and if it wasn't for the thought of leaving Kev behind to fight this thing on his own, I really think I might have taken it.

'When I heard I had terminal cancer, I was so sad to be leaving you and your father, Kevin, but I was so relieved that I could finally stop fighting. I thought when I died, he would die with me, or at least go back to whatever God forsaken place he came from. Obviously, I was wrong about that.

'Since I started getting weaker, I feel him leave me sometimes. I was so happy to have those un-interrupted hours, but then I found out where he goes. I am so sorry Kevin.'

Tears flood down her face, and Kev stands up, brushing the tears from her face, his own eyes filling up and threatening to spill over. My hand is suddenly cold where he let go of it and I realise I was getting as much comfort from the contact as he was.

'Mum,' he says, his voice quiet, breaking. He fights to stay in control of his emotions. 'Mum, please don't cry. None of this is your fault. You couldn't have known where he was going.'

I don't want to interrupt this moment, but I have to know. I have to know because I can't bear the thought that she has somehow seen what happened earlier. I know this is stupid, irrational, she is bed ridden, but I can't push the thought away. With everything else that is going on here, it seems rational is no longer a measure of what is possible. There is every chance Scurra has shown her, taken one last opportunity to upset her.

'Rose,' I say, 'How did you find out where he was going when he left you?'

'He told me. He came back earlier today. Told me he had been in my son. And that he intended to stay there once I had gone. He taunted me. I fought him down one last time because I had to talk to you two, let you know what was going on. That's when I heard you come in Kayleigh.'

She doesn't elaborate on what he said to taunt her and I don't ask. If he has told her what happened, then maybe this way she can convince herself he made it up to upset her. I'm not confident I could lie convincingly if she asked me what had happened. Instead, I move the conversation to safer ground.

'He killed Emma and Zach.' I hear the way my voice catches on their names. Kev sits back down, his hand on my knee, squeezing. I cover his hand with mine.

'I feared as much when he told me where he has been going. Kevin, you must find a way to fight him.'

I have so many questions. How did she fight him down? What did she do to keep him down once she had him there? Did she have any idea on how to get rid of him?

Her eyes close. With a visible effort, she opens them again, but no sooner does she get them open than they close again.

Quietly, I say to Kev 'Come on, she needs to get some sleep.'

He nods agreement and I go to stand. As I do, Rose takes a loud, rattling breath. I freeze. Fighting until the end she drags in another, but that is it. She is gone.

My mind reeling, I feel a thousand things at once. I am so sad for her, yet happy that her fight is over. I am devastated for Kev and I am terrified for him and for me. And I still have so many unanswered questions.

I feel tears on my face and I look across at Kev.

I see a brief flash of yellow in his eyes and I know it's not him.

His eyes fill with tears, and he whispers 'Mum'.

Sliding closer to him, I hold him while he cries. I make all the right noises, but I know it's not him. I am not going to make the mistake of letting on I know though, not yet. Scurra is reacting in the way that he thinks Kev would, he obviously doesn't want me to know it's him. I have no idea why, but maybe me knowing it is will be an advantage.

Rose may not have gotten to tell us how she fought Scurra down, but she did tell us one very important thing. Scurra is frightened of being exorcised. It is possible to beat him that way. I just have to hope that Kev is strong enough to not invite him to stay, strong enough to not give in to whatever desire Scurra promises to grant him.

I will play along until I get a chance to speak to Father Michaels again. I will convince him to help us. I don't know how, but I must and I will.

'I love you Kev' I say against his hair, hoping he can hear me.

Right then, I have never felt so alone. Nor have I ever felt so empowered. Rose's story has given me hope, strength. It's made me see it's possible to maybe beat Scurra, or if nothing else, to hold him at bay. A draw if you like, and right now, a draw seems good to me.

Chapter 10

I don't feel empowered for long. Within minutes I am left feeling as helpless and as out of my depth as I am.

I hear the door open, and taking a deep breath, I turn. I don't know what I am expecting to see – some horrific manifestation of Scurra perhaps. All horns and yellow eyes, or perhaps all good looks and charm. Instead, I see Kev's father. I had been so caught up in the story and what came after that I had completely forgotten about him. I had no idea what to say to him.

This moment would be awkward by any standards, but add to the fact his wife has just died with the added extra that his son is now possessed and where do you go from there?

I feel an urge to laugh. Just laugh at the ridiculousness of it all. That in this day and age, demons are still possessing people, people are still dying far too young, and that I am caught up in the middle of all this instead of out partying and trying to find a hangover cure that actually works. I fight the urge and it passes.

I realise, too late, I am staring at him. Racking my brains for something to say I come up blank. I never know the right words to say when someone has died, but to be actually sat here, the one to have to tell someone their wife has gone. I don't think there are any right words for that.

My hand is mechanically rubbing Kev's back as he stares at the floor, not speaking, the only movement he's making is the gentle up and down of his breathing. I wonder if I should stop. I wonder if I should have covered Rose's face. The things that were running through my mind made those few seconds feel like an hour.

He breaks the silence. 'She's gone hasn't she?'

Dumbly, I nod.

Crossing himself, Daniel walks into the room, and goes to his wife's bedside. He sits down hard in the dining chair placed at the other side of her bed. Taking her hand in his, he lovingly pushes a loose strand of hair back from her face.

'She's still warm,' he comments.

I make a huge effort to pull my tangled thoughts into some sort of order. I have to speak soon; my reaction will surely be registering as abnormal. Then again, perhaps in this situation, there is no normal. Even aside from what I know about Kev, don't a lot of people react strangely to grief? I sure hope so because the last thing I need is Daniel scrutinising my behaviour right now.

With a huge force of will, I put all thoughts of Scurra, even Kev, out of my mind and force myself to say what I think is right.

'Mr Radley, I am so sorry,' I manage. My voice sounds surprisingly normal. A little shaky perhaps but that's ok.

'It's Daniel,' he says absent-mindedly.

'Huh?'

'Call me Daniel.'

'Oh, ok.'

I realise he is as lost as I am on what to say. This gives me a little confidence to continue.

'We were just in talking to her and she died. She told us to tell you she loved you.' This is a little embellishment, but it's what he needs to hear, and even though she didn't use those exact words, didn't ask us to tell him, the fact she made Kev promise not to tell him any of what she told us makes me think this has never been truer.

'Thank you. Did she suffer?'

All her life, I want to say. Instead, I say 'No, she went very peacefully and she spoke of how this would be a relief for her in a way.'

He nodded. 'Thank you.'

He looks over at Kev as though just noticing he is there.

'Are you ok son?' he asks.

Does he look ok? I want to scream. His mother just died in front of him. He hasn't looked up from the floor since you came in. And now he has this thing controlling his thoughts and his actions.

'Look, I should go,' I say instead. 'Leave you two to say your goodbyes, and have some private time.'

I go to stand, but Kev grabs my wrist.

'No,' he says simply, looking up for the first time. I search his eyes, but there is nothing – no sign of Scurra or Kev. They are glassy, lifeless almost. 'Stay.'

'Kayleigh, you are one of the family now and Kevin needs you, you should stay if it isn't too uncomfortable for you.'

I am scared to stay. I don't know how long I can keep up the charade that Kev is Kev. I am scared to let Scurra know I know he's there, and I am scared I say something stupid to Daniel. I can't let Rose down. I can't let Kev down. I am scared I will do both.

'I…' I start. I don't know what else to say. I try again and don't get any further than stuttering out I over again. I try to free my wrist from Kev's hold, but short of peeling off his fingers I can't get loose.

'I'm sorry,' says Daniel. 'I shouldn't have asked that of you, it's too much to put on you. Kevin let her go.'

Kev does as his father says, and my arm hangs uselessly at my side. I feel Kev's eyes boring into the side of my face and I turn my head slightly to look at him. No longer dead looking, his eyes flash with some emotion I can't read. The yellow is definitely there.

I need to leave. I am scared to stay. I realise I am also scared to leave. Scared of what will happen to Kev, scared of what he may do to his father whilst under Scurra's control. Undecided, I stand, dumb, trying to make me feet move.

I am still looking at Kev, trying to read his thoughts somehow, and his eyes flash and the yellow is gone. I can read his emotions now. Scared, sad. He's my Kev again.

'Please, don't go,' Kev says quietly. I throw myself into his arms, holding him, crying, and swearing I will never leave him.

Too late, I remember Daniel is in the room. This must seem like a huge over reaction to someone who doesn't know that sometimes Kev isn't Kev.

I turn to apologise to him, and he shakes his head slightly, a small smile on his face.

How can he not see what is happening here, not sense the dark under tone and awkwardness to all of this. How did he not notice that for the better part of this his son wasn't his son anymore?

I berate myself for being so harsh. His wife just died, I think he's allowed to be a little preoccupied with that.

'Let's go and make some tea,' Daniel says after a long period of awkward silence. Dutifully, me and Kev follow him out of the room and into the kitchen. I take a sneaky glance at my watch and realise that the whole awkward encounter had taken less than ten minutes. It felt like hours.

Sitting around the kitchen table, we sip the tea. Daniel and Kev discuss what Rose would have wanted at her funeral. I sit like a spare part. I want to excuse myself, but I remember the look of helplessness on Kev's face when he asked me stay. I remember promising to never leave him. I stay, concentrating on my cup like all the answers to everything in the universe are in there if I only stare hard enough.

The rest of the day passes in a blur. My head is spinning faster than a waltzer but time seems to have slowed down. This day feels like a whole month.

I reflect on how, in such a short time, I have lost two of my closest friends and now Kev's mother has gone too. And now, I've lost Kev to Scurra. I refuse to let myself think that way. I will get him back. Somehow, I will. I will find a way to get back to Father Michaels. I will make him help me.

After hearing Rose's story, I am determined to get Father Michael's to help me. Scurra has a weakness, and this is it. The Ouija board idea is out of the equation now, he doesn't fear them, they give him power, a way to communicate and further trick me.

Again, I find myself wondering how things could have been different if we had not done that Ouija board. Knowing what I know now, I don't think it would have changed anything for Rose and I think the demon would have still found Kev, but maybe Emma and Zach would still be here. Or maybe it was fate, it was meant to be that way. I don't know and each unanswered question leads to more new ones. I could go crazy thinking this way. I will go crazy if I don't let this go, but it's hard. I have to concentrate on what I do know, and the problem at hand. I can't waste time pondering what ifs.

Somehow, through the course of the day, I have gotten through a visit from the undertaker, who spoke at length to Kev and his father about what would happen next, and a whole lot of funeral plans, ending with him taking Rose away to do whatever it is undertakers do with bodies, a visit from a rather hysterical woman who I was told is Rose's sister, and lastly a tearful phone call with my mother which resulted in her insisting her and my dad come over.

I tried to put her off. She would see something wasn't right here. She would ask too many questions and something would slip. She would have me certified, and Kev would be left to Scurra's wickedness alone.

She wouldn't be put off. She came in a rush of sorry for your losses, and if there's anything I can do's.

We talked for a long time while dad talked to Daniel. I hope dad came up with something better to say that I did, but I find that unlikely.

Mum told me she understands Kev needs me now, but that if it all gets too much for me, I am welcome back home any time I want to go back.

It's weird because everyone around me seems to have just accepted I have moved in here. Kev and I have never discussed it, I didn't really think about it, but it just seems to have happened. If it wasn't for everything that was happening, I would be ecstatic to be living with Kev, but I worry if it wasn't for everything that was happening, maybe I wouldn't be here.

It seems that all the tragedy is what got me here – Zach, Emma, Rose, it didn't seem like either of us wanted to be alone through all of that. Maybe Scurra is making this happen for me. This is a dangerous path of thought, I know that and yet I can't stop thinking about it.

Eventually, my mum and dad left with promises to call and check we were all ok, and more offers of help. I was relieved they didn't notice anything out of the ordinary, yet a part of me wanted to grab them and scream. Couldn't they see I was a mess? How could they not see my world was falling apart? And that Kev wasn't Kev?

How could Scurra make my mum, the person who knew me better than I knew myself, believe everything was ok and normal. I remembered Zach and Emma's funeral, and the strange influence Kev seemed to have over people, making them believe things that sounded extremely far-fetched.

I knew Scurra had to be behind this somehow, his charm making people want to believe him. There was no way I was that good an actress that I could hide all of this alone, especially from my parents. With mounting horror, I realised that I was grateful to Scurra.

Also, I knew I had to get away. I couldn't let my thoughts turn me around to thinking of Scurra as even a tiny bit good. And getting away from him, from Kev, from the whole mess seemed to be the only answer. But I couldn't walk away. I had to stay and find a way to make Kev fight back.

I felt a hand on my knee, and I jumped, startled from my tumbling thoughts.

'You're crying,' Kev says quietly. As I open my mouth to tell him I'm not, I feel the hot tears running down my face.

'Yeah, well it's been a rough day for us all,' I say with a shrug. 'Where's your dad?'

'He went to bed.'

Only when Kev said that did I realise it was after 11pm. I had been lost in my thoughts for hours.

Kev studies my face as I wipe away the tears and fight to get a grip of myself. 'Are you ok Kayleigh?' he asks and the concern in his voice almost sets me off crying again.

'It should be me asking you that,' I respond. I'm not sure if this is Kev or Scurra and I knew then that this was going to be the worst part of it – not knowing who I was talking to. My Kev, or something masquerading as him.

'We're in this together, we look after each other,' he says simply, kissing my forehead. 'Let's go to bed.'

I nod, glad of the chance to switch my brain off, although I fear sleep will be a long time coming.

** *

The day of Rose's funeral dawns bright but with a nip of cold in the air. It's strange, she was always Mrs Radley, until the final hours of her life when she told us the story of her most intimate secret. How could she still be Mrs Radley after that, I feel I know her better than I know most of the people in my life, so now she is Rose.

I look at Kev, asleep beside me, so peaceful looking, so him, and I reaffirm my promise to Rose that I will do whatever it takes to save her son.

I still have no idea how I will do this. How I will be able to slip away and talk to Father Michaels again, how I will convince him to help me, help us, but I know in that moment that I will. I will go to any lengths necessary.

Kev is waking up. Except he's not Kev and he hasn't been since the moment Rose passed away except that one brief moment next to her death bed when he asked me to stay. I know that now. I also know he is still in there, or at least I hope he is.

Over the last week, I have stopped pretending, even to myself. When we are around other people, Scurra plays the role of Kev perfectly. He is warm, caring and lays on just the right level of upset at his mother's death. He's so good, sometimes he almost convinces me that he has gone, and everything will be ok. That it was all a horrible nightmare, or that I had gone momentarily crazy.

When we are alone, the real Scurra comes out. He taunts me, telling me how I will love him more than I ever loved Kev, how we are a perfect team and together we will rule the world. He tells me I am still his favourite and that we will live happily ever after. He tells me of the life we will have together, the children we will raise and how they will be the prettiest, most successful children of their generation. He is seducing me with his words, and the scariest part is I am starting to believe them. I am starting to want the life he is offering me.

He hasn't hurt me, hasn't touched me physically. It's all part of the game. I think he is waiting until I want him so badly, I am begging him for it, then he knows he's got me.

I hope my promise to Rose will keep me strong. A part of me knows that this isn't what I want. That Scurra is charming his way in so he can control us both. He is having his fun with us and nothing more. That part of me grows smaller every day.

I make a silent vow, whether to myself or to Rose I am unsure, that after the funeral, I will deal with this, I will do something. I will find a way.

Daniel is going to stay with his brother and sister-in-law in France for a few days after the funeral. He is lost without Rose and the memories here are too much for him. His brother and sister-in-law have come to stay until the funeral and they have a late flight booked for today for the three of them once it is all over.

He made me promise to take care of Kev while he was gone. I had agreed, how could do anything else? I wanted to scream at him to stay, to notice that Kev wasn't himself, but if even I was starting to buy into the act of Kev, knowing the truth, how could I expect him to notice anything?

Maybe it will be easier with Daniel gone. I can slip away easier. I tried to slip away a couple of days ago, on the pretence I wanted to go and see my family, but Kev said he would come with me. How could I say no without drawing suspicion? I am terrified of what he will do to me without anyone else there though. No, that's not true. I am scared of him. I am scared of myself. I am terrified I will give in, just stop fighting him and embrace the new life he has promised me in his taunts.

Pushing the thoughts aside, I hop out of bed and go to the bathroom to get ready for today. Today is about Rose and whatever happens, I intend to pay my respects to a woman who was stronger than I ever suspected, and stronger than I will ever be.

I purposely leave the room before Kev is fully awake. My immediate plan is to make sure I am not left alone with him. He can't get into my head in a room full of people, he has to keep the act up.

I get ready quickly and tell Kev I will meet him in the main house, slipping out quickly in case he tries to stop me. He makes no move to stop me, just nods agreement and heads for the shower. He knows I can't go anywhere today. How could I explain walking out now, right before the funeral.

Pacing the floor, I make small talk with Daniel and the other family who are here waiting for the cars to arrive.

Kev walks in, dressed in a black suit, white shirt and black tie. I can't help but notice how good he looks, and I feel a stirring in my lower abdomen. Disgusted with myself, I look away from him, but not before he smirks knowingly at me.

He walks over and puts his arm around me. 'Thank you for being here for me today Kayleigh,' he says loudly enough for his family to hear.

I am saved from having to try and form a response by a knock at the door. The funeral director is here, and all conversation stops.

The only sound on the drive to the church is the occasional sniffle and the traffic around us. I stare blankly out of the window, not really seeing anything.

Part of me hopes Kev is in there somewhere, saying goodbye to his mother, and part of me hopes he isn't so he is spared the ordeal of today.

We pull up at the church, the pall bearers opening our car doors, and climb out.

I have a horrible moment where I think Kev won't be able to walk in, that he will burn or something. I know it won't happen, after all, Scurra had no problem taking over Kev through Zach and Emma's funeral in this exact same church.

Of course, things like that only happen in the movies. This thing knows as well as I do that there is nothing sacred or special about a church – it's just a building, bricks and mortar. The power comes from belief, from faith, something Scurra and I both lack.

We enter without any fuss, my arm through Kev's and we walk to the front, to the pews reserved for Rose's close family. The church is full. Rose had a lot of friends and neighbours and they have all turned up today to show their love for her.

Funerals have always fascinated me. People say they are for the dead, I believe they are for the living, our futile attempt to somehow cheat death in the only way we know how, by remembering the life of the deceased. The last chance to say goodbye, even though we know in our heart of hearts they have already gone.

As I ponder this, a plan starts to form in my head. I don't know if it will work, but it's the best I have and I will have to make it work.

'Why are you smiling?' Kev hisses in my ear, his irritation apparent that I have stopped playing my role. I don't feel disrespectful. If I am wrong, and Rose is here somehow, I think she would appreciate my plan, and would be grinning with me.

'I was just thinking of the beautiful life we will have together once this is over,' I whisper back, running my nails lightly and provocatively along his forearm where my hand rests.

As I say it, I notice a woman in the crowd giving us a disapproving look. I want to give her the finger, but I hold back. She doesn't know my inappropriate behaviour is leading to me saving Kev.

I raise my voice slightly as I say 'It'll be ok, you'll get through this,' and the disapproving look turns to one of slightly ashamed concern. I would like to think my acting skills have gotten better, but if I am honest, I know it's more about Scurra's influence than anything I may have said or done.

I could drag Kev up to the altar, rip his clothes off and ride him on top of his mother's coffin and his influence would get crowd approval. It's a scary thought, how influential is, made scarier by how attractive I find it.

As we take our seats, I ask Daniel if he is ok to distract myself from my thoughts. He nods and gives me a tight smile. He looks anything but ok, the strain showing on his face and I see he looks ten years older. I hope his time in France helps him to come to terms with what's happened. More than that, I hope when he returns, his son will be his son again.

The priest begins talking and the shuffling noise of the crowd dies down to silence, broken only by Rose's sister weeping.

The priest doing the service isn't Father Michaels, and I wonder briefly how that came about. It hardly seems to matter when compared to everything else I have to ponder.

This new priest keeps looking at Kev, and I wonder if he sees what only I see. As I watch, I see only admiration on his face as he continues to throw Kev glances and I realise even the priest is taken in by him. It makes me wonder how many of his own words the priest truly believes and how much is just a job to him.

Father Michaels saw what I saw, his faith allowed him to see it. This priest is just reading from a script, playing his part, as much an actor as I am.

Listening to the words, I don't care if the priest believes them or not. He is offering comfort to the people who do believe them. I find myself moved by the eulogy and it hits me that I miss Rose, more than I thought I would. She could have been my one true ally in all of this, but more than that, she welcomed me into the heart of her family and made me feel comfortable there.

I repeat my promise to her in my head. I owe her this and I intend to pay up.

The funeral and the wake pass without incident. The right people say the right things, and leave at the right time. It occurs to me again how this is more about the living than the person we lost. It is like a carefully orchestrated play. One we have performed time and again, and we all know by heart. We watch for our cues and say our lines, hoping our performance is enough to make others feel some emotion, or at least to make them think we are feeling the "right" feelings.

After what feels like another very long day, Daniel says his good byes and leaves with his family to catch their flight to France. That is our cue to leave too. We go around the remaining people, thanking them for coming, and they throw platitudes at Kev about how Rose was a lovely woman, how she will be missed, and of course that she was taken too young, she's in a better place now and she is out of pain. We exit stage left and make our way home.

As we remove our jackets, I wonder how to start the plan. It isn't long before I get my lead in. Kev goes to the kitchen and returns with two glasses of wine. Handing one to me, he holds his up.

'A toast,' he says. 'To leaving the past behind us and looking to the future.'

Something tells me he isn't talking about Rose. He is getting stronger and if I don't get this right, Kev will be gone forever.

'Cheers,' I say, clinking my glass against his and taking a sip. He takes the glass from my hand and places it on the coffee table. He puts his hands on my shoulders, and looks into my eyes. He pulls me towards him and kisses me hard. I kiss him back; I am completely under his spell.

'Kayleigh, no! Fight it!' A voice. Rose's voice. I don't know if it's real or if it's just in my head but it works. It breaks the spell and I pull back.

'Wait,' I pant.

He looks at me questioningly. 'Wait?' he queries. His voice dangerously calm. I have only one chance at getting this right.

'I need to say goodbye to Kev,' I say. 'Please, I want this, I want you, but if it wasn't for him, this would never have happened. I need to say good bye.'

He looks unswayed. A demon can't be swayed by human emotion I tell myself. Think. Play to his ego.

'I want to thank him for bringing you into my life.' He's not budging, the only change to the eerie calmness on his face is slight amusement.

I have to make this work, but I have to be careful not to over play it.

I improvise. 'I don't expect you to understand.'

It seems to work. He won't allow me to think there's anything he doesn't understand.

'I do understand, Kayleigh, I understand all too well. You want to wave this in front of his nose, let him see what he's lost.'

No, totally wrong and not what I was going for at all, but if it's working, I will run with it.

I hang my head in mock shame. 'Does that make me a terrible person?'

His finger under my chin, he gently pushes my head up and I let him. 'It makes us a perfect match. Five minutes.'

Kev throws his arms around me, holding me so tight I think I will burst. I hear him inhale the smell of my hair, and then his lips are on mine. Gentle, loving. And it's really him. My Kev. We kiss for a long time, our tears mingling.

Reluctantly, I pull back. Five minutes isn't long. 'Kev,' I say urgently. 'I'm sorry, I'm sorry about your mum, about this, about everything, but we don't have much time. How much do you know?'

'I see and hear everything, I just can't make you hear me,' he responds. He looks so dejected. How can I do this to him? I know I have to though. I'm bringing him back I remind myself.

'Know this. Know I love you, more than I can begin to tell you now. But it's not enough. Not now. Not after I have seen what I could become with Scurra.'

He doesn't know what I'm planning, that this is all a ruse. His face crumples, his shoulders sag. I want to hold him, tell him everything, make him see what I am doing, but I can't. Scurra may be letting him talk to me but I am not naïve enough to pretend he isn't in there. Watching. Listening.

'I'm sorry,' I finish. Then I turn and run, not waiting for an answer. I have wasted too much of my time already.

I hear Kev shout after me, 'But I love...' the rest is cut off by an angry shout. Scurra is back and he knows I tricked him. He doesn't know the full extent, of that I'm sure, but he knows I used my chance to run from him. I can only hope that Kev can fight him off for a few minutes, buy me some time.

Running blindly, I rely on instinct to take me to Father Michaels' church. Somehow, it works and I heave open the heavy door and run down the central aisle, my head turning frantically left and right, trying to spot him. A few people are scattered around the pews in silent prayer. They turn to stare at me as I run by, dishevelled and crying. All but one hurridly stand and leave. I must be quite the sight.

Reaching the altar, I realise the one person who didn't leave was Father Michaels. He hurries towards me. 'Kayleigh, what it is? What's wrong?'

He remembers me. I feel a moment of relief; it will save a lot of time not having to explain all of the story again. Stupid, how could he forget me. I'm sure it's not every day he gets someone in with stories of Ouija boards and demonic possession.

'Father, you have to help me. He's got Kev, and he's not going anywhere. Please. I know you say you can't do an exorcism, but you can. Only you can help me.'

'Kayleigh, calm down. I have already explained I can't do an exorcism. The bishop would never allow it. Let's...'

I don't let him finish. 'Screw the bishop, we need you.'

The shock on Father Michaels' face stops me.

'I'm sorry Father, I shouldn't have said that but I need your help. We need your help. We have nowhere else to turn. Please, I am begging you. Help us.'

I see his resolve start to weaken. 'Tell me everything that's happened since we last spoke.'

I do. I hold nothing back, not even the bits I am ashamed of. When I finish I feel oddly calm. Something about Father Michaels has that effect on me.

Father Michaels has listened in silence to everything I have said, his face showing shock at times, sorrow at others, but no real indication on whether or not I am swaying him.

'Father, please,' I whisper.

'Ok, I will help you, I will perform an exorcism,' he says. I throw my arms around him, tears of relief pouring down my face. I'm pretty sure hugging a priest is inappropriate, but I don't care. He lets me hug him for a moment, then disentangles himself. 'From what you have told me, it is important to start this as soon as possible. Even if somehow persuaded the Bishop to let me do this, it would take weeks, months even.'

I feel he is talking more to himself than to me and I let him carry on thinking out loud. 'I am a man of God, and I strongly feel God has led you to me. I have to help you, how can I face my judgement when the time comes and tell God I turned you away when you needed me.'

Serious suddenly, he turns to me 'The Bishop can never know about this.'

I nod mutely.

'Don't get your hopes up Kayleigh,' he cautions. 'I have a lot of doubts that this will work, I only know I have to try.'

'I believe in you Father, thank you so much,' I say.

'I'm pleased you do Kayleigh. You will have to trust me 100% and do anything I say without question if this is to have any chance.'

'Anything,' I agree without a second's hesitation.

'Then we will attempt this first thing in the morning. You will stay in my guest room tonight.'

Before I get chance to protest, Father Michaels holds up a hand to silence me.

'This demon knows what you are planning. It's possible you tricked it into letting Kev through for a minute, even if that's the case, it knows now. It's more likely it knew all along and it wants to play with you. It is arrogant enough to believe it has nothing to worry about. It won't come looking for you, it will still be there tomorrow. I have much preparation to do Kayleigh, this can't be rushed. Be ready to leave at 10am tomorrow.'

I have questions, so many questions, I feel like I am constantly in the dark. There is so much happening around me that I just don't understand, but I daren't ask.

I am afraid Father Michaels will think I don't really believe in him and will change his mind. I am afraid if I know too much, fear will paralyse me and I will run away from it all. I only nod agreement and follow him as he shows me to the guest room.

Chapter 11

9.55am. I wait anxiously for Father Michaels to appear, pacing the street in front of the main door to the church.

What if he has changed his mind? I have resisted the urge to go to him all night. Needless to say, I didn't sleep well. I tossed and turned, worrying, wanting to go get Father Michaels and do this sooner, but I kept telling myself he had preparations to do, that he had to do this right.

I eventually drifted off around 5am, but I soon jumped back awake, my sleep plagued with nightmares, and horrible images.

9.57am. I will go and look for him if he isn't here by 10.01am.

I hear the door open and there he is. I do a double take. He is wearing jeans and a white t-shirt and looks so un-priest like that at first I didn't realise it was him.

'Ready?' he asks.

I nod, stopping pacing and walking toward him. As I get to him, he starts walking beside me. I indicate the bag he is carrying. 'Are your robes in there?'

He laughs, but it is a nervous laugh. 'No, I only wear the robes for official business. This is totally off the record.' He notices my expression.

'Don't look so worried. Think of the robes as a uniform to show I am working. It is what's in the heart that counts at an exorcism, not what I am wearing.'

He stops walking. I am a few steps ahead of him before I realise and I turn back. 'Before we go any further I need a promise from you that whatever happens today, you tell no one. I am putting my entire life's work on the line here. I know we discussed this briefly last night, but I need to know you understand that you can't tell anyone about this. It can never become a tale you tell at dinner parties or to your grandkids'

'Of course,' I agree. 'I just want to get this over and forget the whole thing happened.' The mention of grandkids eases my nerves a little. He believes there will be a future. A future where we look back on this as an interesting anecdote.

'Ok. Then let us proceed.'

We walk in silence for a while, each of us consumed by our own thoughts. He breaks the silence.

'I'm sorry we have to walk. I can't involve my driver in this'

'It's fine,' I respond. I would crawl if I had to, and truth be told, the walk is a relief, something to do other than fidget.

'What do you know about exorcisms Kayleigh?'

I think about what he has asked me. What do I know about exorcisms? I decide to be straight with him. This is never going to work if I can't tell him the truth.

'Only what I've seen in the movies,' I admit sheepishly.

'Ok,' he nods. 'Well, let me tell you, it will be nothing like that. There will be no green slime, no talking in tongues and none of the theatrics.'

He sees my shocked expression and smiles. 'Priests watch movies too,' he says.

He continues. 'We will pray. We will ask the Lord to save the innocent soul from this creature, and the Lord will cast him out.'

'It sounds kind of simple,' I say.

'Not simple as such, just not theatrical. The demon will try to charm us, maybe he'll get a little angry, but ultimately, the Lord will prevail.'

'I don't mean to be rude Father, but that sounds a little naïve,' I respond.

'Indeed, to a non-believer such as yourself, it probably does,' he agrees.

'How can you be sure it will work?'

'I can't be sure. I just have to have faith that the Lord will come to us in our hour of need. I asked you before to have faith Kayleigh, I see that made little impression on you.'

I go to speak but he continues.

'I ask you now for something simpler, something I hope you can do. I ask you to have faith in me.'

I realise I can do that. I already have faith in Father Michaels. Mostly because he sees through Scurra, but also because he somehow radiates a quiet calmness.

'I can do that Father.'

'Good.'

We walk the rest of the way in silence, and for the first time in as long as I can remember, my thoughts are untroubled. I have put my faith completely in Father Michaels, and I am trusting him with my life, my future. It should be scary as hell, but it's not.

We reach the house and walk down the driveway, approaching Kev's place. As my hand reaches out and I go to turn the door handle, Father Michaels stops me.

'This is your last chance to go back. To walk away from all of this and start a new life somewhere.'

I shake my head no.

'Ok,' he says. 'Then remember what I said to you last night. You must do anything I ask of you, no matter how strange it seems or how scared you are, quickly and without question. Can you do that?'

'Yes,' I confirm.

'Then go ahead.'

I open the door and we step inside.

'Kev?'

He's sitting on the couch, he looks so calm, so normal, that for a minute I allow myself to believe it's really him. That he beat Scurra on his own. The delusion doesn't last long.

'Hello Father,' he says with casual unconcern. 'I was wondering when you would show up.'

'Hello Kevin,' says Father Michael.

Kev laughs, 'Why don't we drop the act. We both know Kevin is long gone.'

'Then why don't you introduce yourself?'

'You can call me Scurra.'

'That's not your real name.'

'Come now Father, give me a little credit, I'm not going to make it that easy for you. Now, where are my manners? Why don't you set your little props up on that table over there and we can get started? I do enjoy these little games.'

I'm not sure if Father Michaels was expecting that, but if he wasn't he covered it well.

'As you wish,' he said. He crossed the room to the table and from his bag he took a bible, a crucifix, some rosary beads, two candles and a flask.

I stood in the doorway, uncertain what I was supposed to do. Should I help? Father Michaels seemed to sense my feelings. 'Why don't you sit down and make yourself comfortable Kayleigh,' he said without turning around.

Comfortable, that was a joke. There was nothing about this making me feel comfortable, but I sat down anyway. Choosing a chair that faced slightly away from where Kev remained sitting on the couch, I turned sideways so I could see him properly. He smiled at me. All charm again.

Father Michaels finished arranging his things on the table. Lighting the candles and picking up the rosary beads, he turned to face Kev.

Quietly, calmly, he began 'Hail Mary, Mother of Grace, Our Lord is with thee…'

Unperturbed, Kev spoke over him. 'I think you would be pleased to know I am in the process of converting Kayleigh into believing in your friend. At least I assume that's why she yells oh God over and over when I'm fucking her.'

I feel my face burning hot. I want the ground to open up and swallow me. 'Kev,' I start.

'I am not Kev, you shall address me as Scurra,' he snarls. He's getting angry now. 'Who are you to deny me! I will fuck you so hard like the whore that you are while your priest friend watches.'

His words disgust me, yet I feel a rush of wetness flood me, and a wave of desire goes through me, so strong I shudder. I hope Father Michaels mistakes it for a shudder of fear or disgust.

'I thought we were in this together,' I say, desperate to change the subject.

'So did I, but you have shown where your true loyalties lie by bringing him here.' He waves a hand in Father Michaels' direction. 'You have insulted me, and once I have my fun with him, I will finish him off and show you what happens to disobedient girls around here. I may show a little lenience, after all, you have brought me someone to play with, and I do love a good game. If I am completely honest, I like that defiant little spark in you. It turns me on.' He winks as he says this, and again I am torn between repulsion and desire.

I glance over to Father Michaels who is just finishing up his Hail Mary prayer. Throughout the whole exchange, he continued to pray, never losing track, never faltering and his voice unwavering.

'Silence, Demon!' he demands. 'You will speak only to me.'

Kev smirks insolently, but he obeys for the moment.

Father Michaels picks up his bible. Crossing himself, he begins speaking to Kev, in what I think might be Latin. Kev watches him, his attention unwavering. Barely blinking.

Father Michaels is anything but quiet now, his voice booms out, loud and powerful and for the first time, I allow myself to hope this is going to work. He continues to pray in Latin.

He puts the bible down and reaches for the flask. He unscrews the lid and as he reaches the end of the prayer, he dips his fingers in and flicks the liquid onto Kev. I realise as he does this it must be holy water. Some things are the same as the movies I guess.

As the water comes into contact with Kev, he throws his head back and screams, an unearthly sound of pain and torment. He is writhing from side to side, foam forming on the edges of his lips. I can't take it.

I stand and move towards him. 'No!' Father Michaels yells, gesturing for me to remain where I am. I fight every instinct I have and sit back down.

Kev's head comes back to its normal position, he is gasping for breath and his eyes are blood shot, rolling in their sockets. He glares at Father Michaels as he gets his breathing under control.

I hear a small 'Oh' sounds escape me. I don't know how much of this I can take. My Kev is still in there somewhere, maybe feeling this pain.

Father Michaels again flicks the holy water onto Kev, and the reaction is instant. The scream this time is louder, and more pain filled than the last. His head is thrown back in agony again, his eyes bugging out of their sockets, and all the tendons in his neck standing out. His hands form claws and dig into the cushions of the sofa, his feet pedal rapidly a couple of inches off the ground. I swear I can smell burning, although I think that could be my imagination.

'Father, please.' I cry out, standing again, 'enough.'

'Sit,' he orders.

I don't. I move towards Kev, and Father Michaels steps forward and grabs me, pushing me back into the chair. 'Remember what we talked about.'

'I'm sorry. I just can't.'

'Kev isn't feeling this, it is only the thing, the demon who will feel it. Holy water only hurts the unholy.'

I want to run from the room but I am too afraid to move. I am afraid for Kev, I know Father Michaels said he won't feel it, but what if he does? Maybe a little pain, or a lot of pain, will be worth it to get his life back.

Again, mercilessly, Father Michaels flicks holy water onto Kev. He doesn't even wait for him to recover this time. Kev continues to scream and writhe and I wonder how much more of this his body can take.

Sweating now, Father Michaels continues to flick the water, yelling as he does so 'I command you Demon, to leave this son of God. Go back to Hell and walk among demons, you are not welcome on God's Earth.'

Picking up the crucifix, he continues. 'I command you to leave. In the name of the Father,' he thrusts the crucifix towards Kev, flicking more holy water, eliciting another scream, 'The Son,' again a thrust, a flick, and a scream, 'And the Holy Ghost.' A third time. More Holy Water. 'Amen.'

He lowers the cross, panting, spent, and puts the flask back on the table.

'Amen,' he breathes quietly, almost an afterthought.

I look across at Kev, he is no longer screaming, and his fingers have relaxed out of their claw shape. His head droops onto his chest, eyes closed. I look questioningly at Father Michaels, and he nods.

'Kev?' I say quietly.

His head shoots up and his eyes fly open. He laughs. A warm, happy laugh. My Kev is back. Father Michaels did it!

The illusion doesn't last long. 'That was fun,' he says. 'What's next? How about pressing the crucifix against my forehead?'

Father Michaels looks lost, so disheartened, and I know then this is far from over.

'Aww,' says Kev with mock sympathy. 'You really believed it was working didn't you?'

Silently, Father Michaels turns walks towards the door. As he reaches it, he looks back 'I'm sorry Kayleigh, I tried.' He continues walking, crossing the lawn, he means to leave.

'Father, wait,' I cry, jumping up and following him out. 'Please wait.'

He pauses half way across, then continues.

'Please!' I say again.

He turns to me. 'I'm sorry, he is too powerful, it would take a much more experienced priest than me to beat him.'

'But what about what you said to me? You have to have faith, Father, surely your God wouldn't abandon you now just because you don't have experience? Why would he lead me to you if he didn't think you could do this?'

'It seems I was wrong,' he says sadly.

I hear Kev's laughter in the background. I take a couple of steps, bringing me level with Father Michaels and I look him square in the eyes. 'Father, you must see what's happening here. The demon is making you doubt yourself, doubt your faith. You can't let that happen.'

The irony of me trying to convince the priest to believe in a God I don't believe in is not lost on me, but now is not the time to worry about the morality of it, I just have to hope it works.

He laughs. 'That's easy for you to say, you didn't have faith in the first place.'

'But I did Father, I had faith in you – and I still do.'

That seems to do the trick. I see something harden in Father Michael's eyes. 'Then let's begin again tomorrow.'

'No! You've seen how powerful that thing is getting, we can't wait another day. We just can't.'

'The exorcism ritual takes it out of me Kayleigh, normally, we rest for a couple of days after performing it. I am exhausted. I can't do it now.'

'Oh, but you must Father, you must. It's our only hope.'

He nodded, resigned. 'You're right. Let's do this.'

'Well, well,' Kev says as we come back in, me resuming my former position, and Father Michaels moving towards him. 'I wasn't expecting round two so soon. Forgive me if I just sit and ignore you, I thought I would have more time to plan the next show.'

The cocky grin tells me he isn't afraid in the least. I try to tell myself its just bravado. I'm not convinced, and I can see Father Michaels looks beaten already.

Trying not to show my fear, I sit back in the chair and wait for Father Michaels to begin.

It starts in pretty much the same way. Father Michaels say the rosary and reaching for the Holy Water, begins the Latin prayer. As he works himself up into a frenzy, scattering his Holy Water around, true to his word, Kev sits, unmoved. He watches Father Michaels with seeming interest, the sort of interest a huge dog might have watching a tiny kitten trying to scratch it.

As he reaches the end of the Latin, he collapses, his knees giving way, throwing him to the floor, his Holy Water spilling. I jump to my feet.

'You killed him!' I accuse Kev.

'No,' he replies, with the same casual interest, 'not yet. He fainted.'

Not knowing what else to do, I pick up the crucifix and wave it in Kev's direction. I try to remember the words Father Michaels used.

Kev laughs. 'Really? It didn't work for the priest and he actually believes this stuff. If God didn't help him, he's hardly going to help you.'

Much as I don't want to admit it, he has a point, but I can't give up. Not when we have come so close.

Suddenly, I know what I have to do. I don't have faith in God helping me, but I do have faith in what Rose had told me. I will do it her way. I will take Scurra into me and fight him. Once Father Michaels wakes up, we can cast him out together.

I put the crucifix down and walk over to Kev. I sit on the arm of the couch and casually twist a piece of his hair in my fingers.

'I remember when you said I was your favourite. It's me you want. Leave Kev and come with me. We truly can rule the world that way.'

Again, that laugh. 'You think you can fight me don't you?'

Angry suddenly, the truth comes out. 'Yes, I do, and the fact you are too scared to leave Kev and come for me tells me you think I can too.'

'A challenge. How quaint.'

Before I have a chance to respond, I feel something strange. Something like nothing I have ever felt before. I feel something pushing its way into my body through my chest, my stomach. Taking a deep breath, I stop resisting, and it's done. Scurra is in me!

I feel his power surging through my veins, lighting me up. In that moment, I feel like I could take on the whole world and win.

I know I must fight it, although part of me, a dark part I would like to pretend doesn't exist, thinks I could have the best of both worlds here. I could be with Kev and be powerful too. As I feel the power trying to wash over my brain, take it over, I resist it and the push becomes lighter.

I can hear Scurra's voice in my head. It's so strange, like having an alien in my body with me, a parasite. 'Let me in Kayleigh. Let me in, you won't regret it. I will grant you your every desire, anything and everything you want will be yours.'

'I only want Kev,' I think back to him. This feels weird. It's like talking to myself but not all at the same time. 'I don't need you.'

'Oh, dear sweet Kayleigh, you need me more than ever if you want to keep him, though why you do is beyond me. He is weak!'

'I love him.'

'His deepest desire was to have you out of his life, but he was too weak to want to upset you. Why do you think I allowed you to go get that priest? Once you saw there was no hope of Kev coming back, you would have left. You think you wouldn't but you would have. I would have granted him his darkest desire.'

'You're lying,' I shoot back, but even I can feel the uncertainty in my thoughts. What if it was true?

'Maybe, maybe not. Can you afford to take that chance after everything you've risked to be with him? While I'm here, you get to keep him. Let me in.'

I made a split second decision. I would let him in enough to do that, but nothing else.

'OK.'

I relax my mind a little and I feel him come further in.

'Kayleigh, are you ok?' Kev, the real Kev, asks.

I blink and I'm back out of my head and in the room. 'Yes, yes I'm fine.'

'Showtime,' says Scurra. 'I'll make them believe I've gone.'

'Is it really you?' I hear myself ask. This isn't what I expected. I thought it would be very much me and then an alien entity, something very separate from me, but this is more of a merger. I can feel herself welding to Scurra and him to me – and I kind of like it.

Before he can answer, Father Michaels lets out a groan and sits up.

'Father,' I exclaim. 'You did it! Kev's back! Thank you.'

I throw my arms around him. When I let go, Kev helps him to his feet.

Still disorientated, it isn't that hard to convince Father Michaels he did it. It's always easy to convince someone something is true if they want to believe it.

I figure the easiest way is to let him chat to Kev, make him see Kev is who he should be now. I go to the kitchenette to make Father Michaels some tea.

As the kettle boils, I think of how much faith I put in Father Michaels. He is weak, I was wrong to believe in him. I feel contempt when I think of him, and my mouth twists into an ugly sneer.

This isn't me. I don't feel this way. This is Scurra, making me feel this way. I question what I have done, why I thought it was a good idea, but then I remember. Scurra can make Kev stay with me.

Do I want him to stay with me because something makes him? No, of course I don't. I must tell him.

The kettle clicks off and on auto pilot, I make the tea as I debate how I will tell him what's going on.

Scurra's voice speaks to me. 'He won't stay because I make him stay, he will stay because I will make you hotter, stronger, powerful, irresistible.'

That sounds pretty good, I must admit.

I decide I will sleep on it, and see how I feel tomorrow. Having a demon inside you sure does lend itself to bad decision making.

I take Father Michaels his tea and convincingly fawn over how wonderful he is, how he beat the demon and how grateful I am. He buys it all, which does nothing to help change my new opinion of him. No, not my opinion of him, Scurra's opinion of him. Our opinion? Maybe that's it, our opinion. Again, I realise I like this weird merger.

I feel more alive than ever before.

It seems to take Father Michaels an age to drink the tea. It is all I can do not to shout at him to hurry up. I control the urge to yell and let him get on with it.

Eventually, he is done with it. I call him a taxi and hide my impatience as I wait for it to arrive.

Finally, a beep outside. It's there. I thank Father Michaels again, and open the door for him. As the taxi pulls around the corner and out of sight, I breathe a sigh of relief, and head back to the lounge where Kev is waiting.

I sit down beside him. My Kev, the one thing I've ever wanted. He puts his arm around me and I rest my head on his shoulder.

'Thank you K,' he says into my hair, planting a kiss on the top of my head. 'I love you.'

'I love you too,' I say.

I feel sick at the thought of how much I am deceiving him, but I can't risk losing him. I can't.

Chapter 12

I wake up and look over at the clock. It's exactly 3am. Whereas before this would have unnerved me, now I smile. The Devil's hour is my hour now.

Something woke me but I'm unsure what. I lay in the darkness, Kev sleeping beside me, and strain my ears listening for a noise, movement, anything that could have woken me.

I feel a pulsing between my legs. It starts off gentle, nice, and builds in intensity until I can't stand it anymore. I remember now. This is what awoke me.

It is driving me crazy with need. I roll towards Kev as the next wave hits me. He is laying on his stomach, his head turned towards me.

I run my finger nails down his back and whisper his name. He stirs slightly, and louder, I say 'Kev, are you awake?'

He reaches out and puts his arm around me, snuggling into me and muttering something unintelligible. His breathing evens back out.

As I go to wake him, something stops me. I don't want to make love. The need I feel is rawer than that, something more primal.

Gently now, being careful not to wake him, I move his arm and creep out of bed. I move into the centre of the room. In one fluid motion I push my panties down and kick them away.

My clitoris is throbbing in a way I have never felt before. If I don't touch it, I will explode.

Standing where I am, I push my fingers into the warm wetness, roughly rubbing at my clitoris. It feels intense, too intense, but so good. The moonlight streams in, lighting my naked body. I feel exposed, I should feel vulnerable, but I don't. I feel powerful, unbeatable and I don't care who can see me.

As I continue to work my fingers in a circular motion, feeling my orgasm building, I know this isn't me. I am not touching myself. I have given in, I have let Scurra touch me, and I am glad I did.

I have never felt anything like this. My whole body is alive, every nerve ending sending pulses of pleasure through me. I know I made the right choice taking Scurra into me.

When I cum, I cum hard. Harder than ever before, harder than I ever thought possible. As I feel the rush of heat and wetness flood my thighs, my knees buckle and I fall to the ground.

I barely notice and it does nothing to stop me.

Plunging my fingers deep into myself, I throw my head back, supporting myself on my other hand, arching my back, twisting in ways I didn't know I could. My hair hangs behind me in sweaty, damp strings, the sweat stands out in beads all over my body, my skin glistening, hot.

Deeper and deeper I push into myself, feeling the waves building again. I need more, I need to get deeper. Faster and faster, my hand a whirl of movement, I feel the moans being wrenched from my lips. They are involuntary and I do nothing to try and silence them. My juices continue to flow, a new spurt with each inward thrust, my hand is drenched and I'm dripping onto the carpet.

I am so engrossed in what I am feeling, my body is a giant nerve ending, it's only purpose is to pleasure me. I don't hear Kev moving, but suddenly the bedside light snaps on and he is stood over me. I sense him standing there and open my eyes.

His face is horror stricken, white, his eyes open and mouth agape. 'Kayleigh, what are you doing?' he exclaims, his voice shaky, all traces of sleep forgotten.

I don't stop. I look up at him, my fingers still moving in and out, my hips thrusting to match them, my moans getting louder as the pressure builds again.

I look into his eyes and utter three words. 'Fuck me, Kevin.' It isn't a request; it is a demand.

'No,' he says, the horror still present. 'Stop it!'

I don't stop. My lips pull back in a sneer as I continue. He snaps into action, kneeling beside me, grabbing my wrist and pulling my fingers out of me. I try to fight him, try to pull my wrist free, writhing and snarling at him.

'Oh my God, Kayleigh, you're bleeding! Stop!' I hear him, but it's as though he is speaking from far away, like I am dreaming and he is trying to wake me up. I push myself back up onto my knees, freeing the hand that was supporting me.

I reach out with the free hand, clawing at him, his hand, his face, anything to get my other hand free. He keeps his grip on my hand, and with his one free hand he fends off the one that is scratching at him.

'Kayleigh, if you can hear me, you have to fight him. Come back to me. Don't let him in.'

Those words break the spell, and somehow, the real me fights back. I use every ounce of mental power I have and push Scurra down, rising back up to take control.

As I get control, I feel my body shaking, I am panting and I can feel wetness on my thighs. This no longer turns me on, I feel nothing but disgust.

Kev is still holding my wrist, my other arm hangs loosely over my thigh, and I look at him. His face is scratched and bleeding like he lost a fight with an alley cat. What have I done? His beautiful face. I feel the tears come and I can't stop them.

Dropping my wrist, Kev pulls me to him, holding me. His warm arms encircle me, and I feel warm and safe. The tears keep coming, huge gasping sobs that wrack my entire body.

'I'm sorry, I'm so sorry,' I repeat over and over like a mantra.

'It's ok,' he soothes, making shh noises against my hair.

I start to feel more in control of myself, and my sobs taper off to hiccoughing gasps, eventually quieting altogether.

Coming fully back to myself, I know I don't deserve Kev's forgiveness and I certainly don't deserve his comfort. I pull back from him, wriggling out of his arms and scooting back a bit.

'It's ok,' he states again.

I shake my head. 'It's not ok. Look what I've done to you.' I reach up and gently touch his face where my nail marks stand out red and ugly, trickling blood. He winces slightly and I pull my hand back, looking down, ashamed of myself.

As I look down, I see blood in the wetness that I can feel drying on my thighs and hand. I have clawed at myself almost as badly as I have clawed at Kev's face.

Between what I have done to myself, and what I have done to Kev, the person I love most in the world, I know Scurra can't offer me what I need. I will fight him. He will never again get to take control of me.

I feel rather than hear him snigger inside of my head. 'Oh, fuck off,' I think back to him. The laughter stops but I am not naïve enough to think that's the end of it.

'You need to get cleaned up, then we will have a talk about what just happened,' says Kev.

I nod and stand, my legs still shaky. I feel a fresh spurt of blood run out from between my legs and I know in that moment no amount of showering can make me feel clean. I leave the bedroom and head for the bathroom without another word.

Standing under the hot faucet, watching the water turn pink as it runs down the drain, I try to put my thoughts in order. It's not easy with Scurra's constant presence. How can I think up a plan to get rid of him when he is part of my thoughts?

I hear him again. 'I am going nowhere. You are not even close to powerful enough to get me out. Your desire for darkness, for pleasure, is too strong.'

I want to deny it, but he is partially right. I feel my hand moving down towards myself again. With a deep breath, I fight it. I pull my hand back and reach for the shampoo.

As I lather my hair, I think back to something my psych teacher in college talked about. She talked about putting feelings into drawers, neatly labelled in your head so thoughts don't mix up and you can forget the bits you don't want to remember. She talked about this being unhealthy and something that psychologists work to eliminate.

I am guessing she never had to deal with something like this. If she did, she would have described it as multi personality disorder. This gives me an idea and I visualise two drawers in my mind. One is labelled private. The other has no label.

I imagine the drawer labelled private being tucked away somewhere in the furthest recesses of my mind. This is where I will do my thinking about how to get rid of him. I have no idea if it will work or not, but I have to try something.

Feeling a little better now I have a plan, even if it is only a flimsy, half plan, I rinse my hair and step out of the shower.

Wearing Kev's bath robe, I go back into the bedroom. Kev is getting up from the floor, a bucket in his hand. He has washed away the evidence of what took place only moments before.

'Alright?' he asks. Biting my lower lip, I nod. 'Come on.' He holds his hand out to me and I take it, following him through the garden and into the kitchen in the main house. He pours the water out of the bucket and returns it to the cupboard under the sink, throwing away the blood stained cloth.

I feel like we are trying to cover up a crime. He must have put the coffee pot on when he came along for the bucket. He gets two cups and fills them, handing one to me. I sip. It's too hot and it burns my lip and tongue but I don't care. It's good to feel something normal.

He sits at the kitchen table, motioning me to join him. As I walk over I look at his face. He has washed the blood away. It doesn't look as bad as I feared, the scratches are mostly surface scratches not the huge claw marks I imagined, but that doesn't make the guilt any easier.

I pull out a chair and sit, wincing. I have put a sanitary pad on to catch the blood that is still slowly trickling from me and it hurts when it presses against me. I see the look of concern on Kev's face and I hate myself.

'What the hell happened up there?' His voice is gentle. I want him to scream and shout at me. That I would understand. This, I don't know how to deal with.

He is waiting for an answer and I have no idea how to start. Instead, I blurt out the first thing I think of. 'Why aren't you mad?'

He reaches across the table top for my hand. 'I know that wasn't you up there. I just want to know what happened. I thought that thing had gone for good.'

Taking a deep breath, I go to my private place and I tell him everything. How I thought Father Michaels was dead, so I took Scurra into me to save Kev because I couldn't think of another way. How I planned to fight him, but I found I actually liked his presence and what he could give me. The whole story flooded out, until I finished up with my private mind drawer.

'Wow,' he breaths when I finished. There are tears in his eyes as he asks 'You took that thing for me?'

I nod not trusting my voice to work.

Pulling his chair round until it is practically touching mine, he looks into my eyes.

'This is what we are going to do. When we finish this conversation, you are going to remove that drawer from your head. It's never going to work; he'll find a way in.'

I nod along but don't interrupt. He's right.

'We are going to go back to bed and first thing in the morning, we will go back to the church and speak to Father Michaels again. We will explain everything and get rid of this thing once and for all.'

Again, I nod. I'm not convinced it will work, I'm worried Father Michaels will turn his back on me after I deceived him, but I am hoping that he will see it wasn't me that did that, it was Scurra's influence.

Whatever happens, it is a relief to let Kev take control. I am tired of fighting, tired of thinking. There is one thing I need to know before I can fully let go though.

'Kev, when I took Scurra into me, I had no intention of letting him get a grip on me. He told me your deepest desire was to leave me, and he could make me attractive enough that you would want to stay.' I want to add on is that true, but I daren't I am too afraid of the answer. Kev answers the unsaid question anyway.

'You know how powerful that thing is, how it can make you believe things. It lied to you Kayleigh. I love you and I never want to leave you.'

I want to believe him so I do. A tiny part of me hears something more – a tremor, a hesitation? I can't put my finger on it, but something wasn't quite right.

The doubt comes from Scurra I reason, he's still in there and he's still working on me.

'You believe that if you want to, but I give it a month without me.' Scurra's voice in my head. I let my guard down too far. 'I'm looking forward to visiting our mutual friend tomorrow.'

I refuse to react to him.

'I love you too,' I smile at Kev.

He stands, and gently helps me up. Taking my hand, he leads me back to his bedroom. He pulls the covers back and I fall onto his bed, suddenly exhausted. He covers me up and gets in beside me, holding me. I can't keep my eyes open any longer and I fall into a deep, dreamless sleep.

***

Sitting in the front pew, Kev holding my hand, it occurs to me that before any of this happened, I would never have been in a church except for the obligatory weddings, christenings and funerals.

I look around me at the stained glass, the crucifix behind the altar and the ornate carvings of religious figures. I wonder how people find comfort in such things. They all depict pain and suffering. Maybe it makes people believe they are not alone, even when they are at their lowest.

Before I have time to ponder this further, Kev squeezes my hand, bringing me back to reality and I realise Father Michaels is talking to me.

'...and I will finish this.'

I have no idea what he has said. 'I understand Father.'

Why did I say that? I don't understand, he could have said anything.

'I wasn't talking to you.' Now I'm really in a hole. He was obviously talking to Kev and I have just made it obvious I wasn't listening properly. 'I was talking to that thing inside you, whatever you think I just said, it lied to you.'

I nod, looking down in a way I hope looks demure but is actually to hide the small smile that is playing across my lips. He thinks Scurra phased me out. There are advantages to this.

A voice inside my head. 'See, we make a perfect team.' Not for the first time, I wish his voice wasn't so hypnotic. The perfect tone, low and masculine, powerful, the sort of voice that makes people take notice.

I ignore the comment.

'What next Father?'

'This demon is strong Kayleigh.' I silently compare Father Michaels' voice to the one in my head. His voice is a bit higher, not as masculine. It doesn't command respect, but there is something to it, a tone, that makes me feel safe, like he has all the answers. It's a voice I could trust, rely on.

Absent-mindedly, I nod. I wonder if they teach that voice in priest school. I wonder if there's such a thing as priest school.

Father Michaels is holding me firmly by the tops of my arms, looking into my eyes. He is shouting. 'You must fight it Kayleigh.'

'Oops,' Scurra.

It hits me. When my mind wanders like that, it's not because I'm distracted. Scurra is taking over, pushing me down. He's slowly taking over me, and I am in the process of letting him. Well no more. I am no pushover and I am not about to start backing down now, no matter how tempting it is or how nice it feels to just stop fighting.

I jump to my feet, almost knocking Father Michaels to the floor. He catches himself. I pace the floor between our pew and the altar. My face scrunched with the effort, I push Scurra down. I can still hear him, but it's like a whisper, an echo. I can ignore this.

'Ok, Father, he's gone. I can hold him down for a while.' I continue pacing. Somehow it's easier to hold onto myself when I physically moving.

'He's strong Kayleigh, stronger than any demon I have encountered. The traditional exorcism wasn't enough. I was naïve enough to believe it had worked, but it showed me his power. He was able to leave Kev and jump into you, right before my eyes.'

'What does that mean for us?' asks Kev. I love that he said us. I feel a warm glow in the pit of my stomach and Scurra's echo is gone altogether.

'Well, it means we have to do something more. A sort of tailor made exorcism if you will. It's risky, but it can be done.'

'Let's do it,' I say.

'First, you must get his name. His real name, not whatever it is he chooses to call himself.'

'How?'

'That's the risky part. You could try to trick it out of him, but a demon this powerful would be almost impossible to trick. You must make a deal with him. You must promise he can live within you, control you for as long as it suits him. In return, you want to know his real name.'

'Why would that work? If he is so powerful, he doesn't need my permission for that.'

'You are pretty powerful yourself. I don't know how you are doing it, but somehow, you are holding him off. He will take the easy road. Demons are lazy creatures. He believes he is unbeatable, but he will choose the easiest path to control you.'

I think back to what Rose said about her exorcism. He took the easy path then, needed or wanted her permission. This could really work.

'If I agree to this, what happens next? If I have given him permission to take over me, I've invited him in. How can I fight him off?'

'Firstly, this is a demon, not a vampire. You would do well to read some scripture rather watching movies. The Lord's word shows us...'

He trails off as he sees my raised eye brow. 'Ok, not the time for a sermon, I'm sorry. My original point still stands though. The demon doesn't work like a TV show vampire. It will still be possible to hold him back, it will just be immensely difficult.'

'It's immensely difficult now.'

'No, it's nothing compared to how hard it will be.'

'Ok, so assuming I agree to this, what if I can't fight him down? What happens then?'

'That is where I need you to trust me. Once I have the name, I will be able to exorcise him. That is why these demons are so hesitant to give out their names. You must be strong, you must promise him the world and make it sound so fantastic, he won't be able to resist.'

'I still don't get it! He is already in me; he can already take over me. Why will he go for this deal? And don't say it's because he's lazy. I know there's something you are not telling me.'

'You're right. There is more to it. If I expect you to trust me, I must be honest with you.'

Pausing, Father Michaels sits down in the pew. A bead of sweat stands out on his forehead, and begins to run towards his eye. He wipes it away and fiddles with his collar. He locks his hands together on his legs, suddenly looking composed.

'Let me ask you something. If I told you I didn't believe that trees existed, would them make them any less real?'

'What's that got to do with anything?' I don't think that look is composure. I think he might be having some sort of breakdown.

'Just answer the question.'

'No, of course it wouldn't make them any less real.'

'Good.' He pauses.

'Good,' he says again more quietly, almost to himself.

'I'm sure you've heard stories about people selling their souls to the Devil. They get their wish granted – money, fame, power – whatever it is they want most in the world. And in their dying minutes, the Devil comes back, takes their soul, and they are damned for all eternity. Right?'

'I've heard them.'

'What do you think of them?'

'This is kind of awkward to admit to you Father, but I don't believe in an immortal soul. When we die, we are gone, simple as that.'

'I figured you would think along those lines, and I appreciate your honesty. It doesn't mean you are right though. Like the trees I asked you about earlier, just because you don't believe in the soul, doesn't mean it doesn't exist.'

So he wasn't having a breakdown. 'Nicely played Father.'

'Indeed. What those stories get right is that the soul is destined for eternal damnation. What it doesn't get right is that the Devil comes back and takes the soul at the point of death. The Devil takes the soul at the instant the deal is agreed on. He is free to take control of the person any time he chooses. I worded my proposal to you in a way I thought you would relate to, but what you have to understand Kayleigh, regardless of how I worded this is that I am asking you to trade your soul with this demon in exchange for his real name.

'That is the hook. That is what he will want, and he will do just about anything to get it. I wasn't lying about his laziness though. He will choose the path of least resistance. I am certain of it. He is arrogant enough to believe that even with his name, once he gets you, I won't be able to expel him. Make no mistake that he can't hear this, but he will take the bait anyway, because he believes himself unbeatable.'

'Ok, I'll do it.'

'That's what I need to hear, but first, you need to think long and hard. If something goes wrong, you will be trapped in a jail cell of your own making for all eternity.'

'I don't believe in....'

Father Michaels jumps to his feet. Gesticulating wildly, he walks towards me. 'Are you really so arrogant yourself that you can't even entertain the possibility that you are wrong? Just think about it for a second. You say you don't believe in an eternal soul, life after death or Heaven and Hell, yet here you are, the living proof. You have a demon inside of you. A demon that has been dead in his earthly form for thousands of years.' His voice is loud in the quiet church, echoing.

Panting, he stops shouting and his arms fall limply to his sides. Calmly, he adds 'At least think about it hypothetically. Imagine eternity, time unimaginable stretching before you. Now imagine you are blackened, a husk of evil and pain, no reprieve. Can you take that chance?'

I sit back down in my original place next to Kev. And I do think about what Father Michaels is telling me. I really do. Religion has always sounded so ridiculous to me. Yet I have to admit Father Michaels has a point. I have something in me, even if it's not a demon in the biblical sense, it's something.

'Why me?' I ask. 'What would this powerful demon want with me? A disbeliever is hardly going to score many points, and I'm not important enough on any scale for him to want me.'

'The demon doesn't need someone powerful, he can make you powerful if that's what he wants. The demon likes to play with people, it's as simple as that. He likes the thrill of bending good people to his will. You might not be religious Kayleigh, but you are a good person, and corrupting that will appeal to him.

'You believe in the power of love, and that love is enough. In fact, it's all that matters. It can beat anything. You see the good in people, and you trust easily. That is the appeal. Taking someone so pure and making them dark, twisted and filled with hate.

'As for being a non-believer, that makes you an easier target in some ways. If you don't believe in eternal damnation, you have nothing to lose, so you are much more likely to agree.'

That makes a certain kind of sense. There is something in Father Michaels' words that makes me believe him. Maybe it's because he isn't trying to make me believe him for any reason other than him wanting me to go into this with my eyes open.

I can't start to believe this now. It will only make it harder. Another good point raised by Father Michaels.

'Why are you telling me this Father? It's like you are almost trying to put me off.'

'I am telling you this because you need to know how high the stakes are. If I tricked you into doing this, then I am as bad as him.'

I know in that moment I can trust Father Michaels. Regardless of what I believe, Father Michaels genuinely believes this stuff and he has told me everything. All the bad parts, all the bits that could have put me off. He didn't have to do that, but he did, because he believed it was the right thing to do.

'I'll do it Father. I'm still not sure how much of this I believe, but I believe in you.'

'No. No, you are not doing it.' Kev says. Up until now, he hasn't said a word. I almost forgot he was there. 'It's too risky. I got you into this mess and I am not letting you do this. Father, there must be another way.'

'There isn't,'

I turn to Kev. 'I can do this. I have to. I need you to believe in me.'

'I do believe in you, but it's too big, there's too much at stake, and I know how powerful that thing is. It took me over completely when I was trying to fight it off. Imagine what it could do if you willingly let it take you. I can't let you do that.'

'Don't you see? It's the only way to get rid of this thing. I have to do it, and I am going to – with or without you. If you can't deal with that, then you should just leave now.'

My heart is in my mouth. I can't do it without him, but I can't do it if he doesn't believe in me to beat this thing. Please stay I silently urge him. I need you.

Tears form in my eyes, but I don't weaken my resolve.

'I'll be by your side all the way,' he finally says.

I let out a breath I didn't know I was holding.

'What now?' I ask Father Michaels.

'Go home. You can't make a deal with a demon on sacred ground. Do whatever you have to do to make the deal. Be careful, listen to every word and make sure it is exactly as we discussed it. Once the deal is struck, he will reveal his name. You won't have much time. You must tell Kev the name the instant you hear it.'

He turns to Kev. 'When the deal is done, you will see a change in Kayleigh. It may be subtle at first, she might act slightly out of character, or it could be a huge leap into someone else entirely. Remember this is not her. The demon will try to trick you. He will try to make you think he is Kayleigh, the demon is gone, you don't need to act. Do no fall for this. The second you have that name, call me.'

He hands Kev a business card. 'That is my private mobile number, I am available 24 hours a day on that line.'

Kev nods solemnly and takes the card. He glances at it, then takes out his wallet and tucks it in behind his credit card.

Even in the middle of this I am fascinated by the fact the priest has a business card to hand out in the same way a lawyer or an insurance salesman would.

'Go now. Call me when it's done. If you need any help in the meantime, call me and I will do my best to advise you.'

'Thank you Father.' I throw my arms around Father Michaels. When this is over, I should really check with him if this is appropriate or not. 'Thank you.'

He hugs me back briefly, then firmly removes himself and walks through a door to the left I hadn't even noticed without another word.

We begin walking towards the exit of the church. Until Father Michaels walked away, I hadn't known it was his presence that was keeping me calm. All the doubts, all the panic begins to rise up in my chest, my throat. I can't breathe.

I cling to Kev. He holds me tightly and he's the only thing that stops me passing out.

'Breathe. Deep breaths. In. Out.'

I follow his instructions and my breathing goes back to normal. My heart rate slows down and I feel a bit more in control.

'What happened? Are you ok?'

The concern in Kev's voice is what I need to gain full control once more. I have to be strong, not someone to be pitied.

I loosen my grip on him. 'I'm fine.'

'You can do this Kayleigh. I believe in you.'

In that moment I know I can do it. I am not going to throw my life away on a promise to a demon. Even if it means losing Kev, I can beat this thing. I can.

Chapter 13

Once I decide I can do this, everything else seems to fall into place. Maybe there's some truth to our minds being so powerful, so open to suggestion, or maybe the plan was there all along, and I just needed to believe in myself to fully see it. Whatever it came about, I went from having no idea how I was even going to begin, to having a plan fully formed in my head.

I know I must do it alone. Having Kev there will be a distraction. I can't allow myself to focus on his safety, or on how worried he will be.

I finish the final sip of coffee and put the cup down on the table in Kev's father's sitting room.

'I'm ready,' I tell him. 'Go wait in the kitchen.'

'You're not doing this alone.'

'Yes, I am.' My voice comes out cold and authorative. I want to hug Kev and tell him everything will be ok, but I can't. I won't be weak any more. I am not going to let emotion get the better of me. 'Go.'

It's not a request, it's a command. Father Michaels' words come back to me. Turning me from someone loving to someone cold doesn't seem much of a stretch any more. I am becoming that person on my own.

No, I reason with myself. I am doing this for love not hate. I think of the promise I made to Daniel that I would take care of Kev, the promise I made to Rose that I wouldn't let Scurra take her son. It feels like it was a million years ago, but when I said I would, I meant it. I didn't think I would be doing it this way, but that's life.

Kev opens his mouth as if to speak. He looks at me and something in the determined set of my face, the tight line of my mouth must put him off.

He walks out of the room, lightly brushing his hand across my shoulder as he passes me.

I gave it a couple of seconds until I guess he must be in the kitchen. Then taking a deep breath, I begin.

'Scurra, are you here?' I ask in my mind. It feels weird talking internally like this.

'Always,' he responds.

It must be weird for him too, or maybe it's a show of power, but instead of answering in my mind as I expected, he speaks the answer out loud. In his voice. From my mouth.

'Don't be so sure. You and me, we need a little talk.' I speak out loud too. Somehow, I keep my voice level.

'Is that so?'

'Indeed it is.'

'And what could you possibly have to say that would interest me?'

'I think you know.'

I know he knows. After all, he is in me. Even though I managed to stay in control back at the church, I could still feel him in me, lurking, listening.

'You want me to fall for your trap. It's extremely disrespectful you know. I'll let it go this time, because it's so amusing that you think you can outwit me.'

How do I play this? He can read my every thought. I haven't thought this through enough.

His scornful laugh bursts from my mouth.

Suddenly, I know what to do. I retreat slightly in my mind, back into my drawer. I told Kev I would erase the drawer from my mind, but I didn't, I only erased the contents. It is so simplistic, yet somehow it works. I can feel that I am alone with my thoughts. He seems to notice too.

'Ok, let's talk. Run me through your little plan.'

His voice is sarcastic, he's humouring me. Talking to me like one would a child. But I hear something else, a tiny waver. Maybe I imagined it, but I think I have caught him on the back foot slightly. Now I just have to play it to my advantage.

'Well, let's see,' I begin. 'I don't like having something in my head that is weak. So weak, it daren't even reveal its name because it's scared of a powerless little priest.'

I am taunting him. It's dangerous, but it feels good.

'I am scared of no one.'

'Prove it. Tel me your name.'

'Nice try. What's in it for me?'

I decide to go off script a little, try a little something he hasn't heard and won't see coming.

'There's nothing in it for you.'

'Then I am bored of this conversation. Cut to the chase while you still have a tiny bit of my attention.'

'You can prove that you are more powerful than the church.'

'Ha! I have nothing to prove to those idiots. The fact I can take one of their so called innocents and turn them completely to my will is proof enough. You are growing more boring by the minute.'

I'm losing him. I don't want to push it too far.

'Ok,' I say. 'I'll give you two choices. Choice one: you can stay, we can work together and become the powerful entity I know we can be. You can take the wheel, make the decisions, do whatever you please, but in return, I get to know the name of the one who can make me a somebody. Or choice 2: you can admit you are too scared to reveal who you really are, and just leave now. No hard feelings.'

'Oh, you're feisty, I'll give you that. We could be great together. But I will ask again, what's in it for me? Choice 2, which we both know is not a real choice, just something you said to try and annoy me, I get nothing. Choice one, I get nothing I don't already have.'

He's playing it clever. I have to trust that Father Michaels is right. That he will want my soul, and can't fully take it without me allowing it.

'What makes you think you already have choice one?'

As I say this, I put every ounce of my mental strength to work. I refuse to allow my mouth to move, my vocal chords to vibrate. He pushes, trying to overcome me. I'm holding him back. I'm actually holding him back! The elation I feel adds to my strength, and suddenly it's not as hard any more. I can do this. I am doing it. He can't beat me.

I push harder and I speak myself. 'What's the matter, cat got your tongue?'

Not the best line, not the line I would have used if I had time to think about it, but not bad considering the situation I'm in.

I hear his scream of rage in my head. It bounces around my skull, it hurts, but I feel victorious, and the pain is secondary.

My right hand flies up and slaps me across the face. Hard.

My ear rings and my skin stings like a burn.

'Stupid girl. You are no match for me.'

I lost focus slightly when he slapped me, and his voice comes from my mouth again. I should be upset, but I'm not. I know it's possible to control him, it will just take more will power.

'Prove it,' I fire back. 'Take the deal.'

'I have proved you cannot outwit me. I have proved you cannot beat me physically or mentally. I need to prove nothing more. If you still think that by not giving you my name, I am showing fear of an irrelevant priest, I have proved you are stupid too.'

Maybe I am stupid, but I don't believe his words. He has proved nothing except that I am a match for him. He has been doing this for thousands of years, I have been doing it for the last day, and already I have held him down for a time.

I shrug. 'Have it your way.'

'That's it, you've given up?'

'Oh, far from it. I'm just taking away your chance to do this the easy way.'

Before he gets a chance to reply, Kev bursts in.

I push Scurra all the way down. This is getting easier. I am adapting. Or maybe he's tired with pushing so hard. That makes me think. What happens when I get too tired to fight him anymore? I can't let myself think like that. Father Michaels will find a way.

'Kayleigh, stop.'

'Kev, what the fuck?' I yell. 'I told you not to come in here. I was just starting to make progress. What is so important it couldn't wait.'

I am so mad I don't hear his reply the first time.

'What is it?' I yell again.

Quietly, Kev says the last thing I expect and the last thing I need to hear. 'Father Michaels is dead.'

'What?' I explode. 'What do you mean he's dead? He can't be dead? He's our only hope! Why do you even think he's dead?'

There are so many more questions, but these are the first ones that come out of me.

'Sit down.'

'I don't want to sit down. I want you to explain to me exactly why you thought bursting in here with made up stories was going to help. I hate you, I really hate you. You want this thing to win don't you?'

Even as I say it, I know it's not true. I am over reacting more than I ever have before, but the thought that Father Michaels might be dead and we are on our own is too much to bear. It's easier to believe Kev is trying to sabotage the plan.

'Kayleigh, it's not made up. Why would I make something like that up?'

He's talking to me like I'm a fragile idiot. It makes me madder. I just fought down a demon, I don't need to be treated like a child.

'Lose the tone,' I hiss, 'and tell me what the hell is going on.'

'I just got a call from a Father Spencer. I don't know who he is, but...'

'He's Father Michaels stand in,' I interrupt.

'Ok, well he told me Father Michaels had passed away. He had a heart attack this morning and died pretty much instantly.'

At that, I do need to sit down. I back up to the couch, and more flop than sit. My mind is racing.

'It's happened again.'

'What do you mean?'

'That's what happened to the priest in your mum's story, remember.'

He sits down next to me. 'Yeah, I remember.'

We sit in silence for a moment. I break it.

'Wait, how did Father Spencer know to call you?'

'He said he went into the library, and found Father Michaels reading. He asked him what he was reading, but he was distracted and dismissed him. He could see something was bothering Father Michaels, so he went to make him a cup of tea. He took it into the library and found Father Michaels collapsed on the floor. He could hear groaning so he went to him. He pulled his phone out to call an ambulance, but Father Michaels told him not to. He said to him that's the way it worked. And he gave him a piece of paper with a number on, my number. He told him to call me and tell me he was dead, and that Father Spencer must finish what he had started. Then he died.'

'Oh my God,' I breathe. 'What did you tell Father Spencer?'

'I hung up. I'm sorry, I panicked. I just knew I had to come and talk to you.'

'Ok, that's good,' I say, my mind racing. In that moment, I don't know much, but I do know I am not involving Father Spencer in this. No one else is going to die because of me.

'Go call him back. Apologise for hanging up, tell him you were shocked.' I'm thinking on my feet now, and ideas are coming to me. 'Tell him Father Michaels was talking about our wedding ceremony, that's what he wanted him to take over. Tell him Father Michaels thought we were a little too young and should maybe wait a year or two, and that we are going to take his advice. Do not tell him any of what's happening.'

'But how's he going to help us. I think Father Michaels was studying up on the exorcism ritual he would use. What if Father Spencer doesn't know it?'

'Father Spencer won't be helping us. No one else is going to die because of this. The church can't help. I'm on my own.'

'Kayleigh…'

'Just do it Kev, I can't have anyone else's death on my conscience. I won't.'

'Ok, but I need you to know, you're not on your own. You've got me. Nothing you can say or do will persuade me otherwise. I'll go and make the call and then we'll work out what we do next.'

'Don't go, call here,' I say. Hearing him say we're still in this together after all I said to him when he came in has made me realise how much I still need him. I thought I could do this without him, but I can't.

As he begins to punch in the number, I put my hand on his arm.

'Wait,' I say. 'I'm sorry about the way I yelled at you. I don't hate you, I love you.'

'It's fine,' he smiles, his hand moving to cover mine. 'I love you too. We'll get through this Kayleigh.'

And just like that I know we will.

In my head I hear faint laughter. 'Now do you believe I'm not weak?'

'Oh, can it,' I respond, blocking out the dying echoes of the laughter.

My mind is already beginning to spin with the thoughts of how I'm going to do this. How I am going to beat this thing on my own. I know I will be spending a long time in my little drawer. Whatever I choose to do, Scurra can't know about it in advance.

'He bought it.' Kev's voice brings me out of my thoughts.

'Huh?'

'Father Spencer. He believed my wedding story. He's glad we want to wait, and he thinks it is a fitting tribute to Father Michaels that we are taking his advice. I feel bad lying to him.'

'It's for his own good. If we drag him into this, it's another death on my conscience.'

'Not your conscience, Scurra's conscience.'

'That thing doesn't have a conscience.'

***

I've spent the last few hours researching exorcisms online. I asked Kev to go out and buy a Catholic bible.

I am armed and as ready as I'll ever be.

I ask myself for the hundredth time if attempting to exorcise myself is even possible, let alone a good idea. The truth is, I don't know, and no amount of debating it will give me a clear answer.

There's only one way to know for sure and that's to try it.

'Are you sure about this Kayleigh', asks Kev.

'Am I it sure it will work? No. Am I sure it's worth a shot? Yes.'

'Just to make sure I understand, you are going to pray for help to someone you don't believe exists, and expect him to bail you out.'

I nod. 'Exactly.'

'How do you think this has any chance of working? If you don't believe in God, who are you expecting to answer these prayers?'

I am fast losing patience.

Sighing, I ask 'Is now really the time for a debate?'

I have never believed in God or organised religion. Kev isn't deeply religious but he does believe in God, and it has led to several heated debates between us in the past.

'I'm not looking for a debate; I just genuinely want to know.'

I relent a little. He has a right to know what's going on. If it all goes horribly wrong, there's a good chance he will be affected by this too.

'Remember when Father Michaels asked if I was really arrogant enough to not even consider that I could be wrong about all of this?'

Kev nods, smiling.

'Well if it was just me that thought it was impossible, he would have a point, but it's not. It thousands of years of learning and scientific advancement that have disproved the notion of a God.'

He rolls his eyes. Unperturbed, I continue.

'Assuming somehow, all of those extremely clever people were wrong and that God exists, I figure he put all that there as a test of our faith. That's a pretty low blow and he owes me some help.'

'You really don't understand how faith works do you?'

'Yes, I understand it. I also understand the logic of eating salad, but I would still rather have a pizza.'

The eye roll again.

'On a less cynical note, if God exists in the way you believe he does, regardless of whether or not I believe he does, he will forgive me and expel this demon.'

'That's a bit simplistic.'

'That's ok,' I say. 'I don't really believe that will happen. What I actually believe is that the words of the exorcism prayer are more a mantra to focus your mind and concentrate your energies on beating off this thing. That's what I actually think will work.'

Kev raises an eyebrow. 'I suppose it's worth a shot.'

Great, even the religious one doesn't believe it will work.

'Let me ask you something. You believe in God right?'

He nods.

'Do you believe in the all-powerful, all loving and forgiving God?'

He nods again.

'Then why don't you think he will forgive me and come to me in my hour of need?'

A frown crosses Kev's face. He goes to speak, but no words come. He tries again, and still no words.

I answer for him. 'Because deep down, when it's on the line, you don't believe in this any more than I do, you just like the idea of it.'

'No, it's not that.'

'Then what is it?'

'I…I don't know.'

'You know what, forget it. We can't afford to be fighting each other now. Let's just do this and see how it goes.'

'You're right,' he says, hugging me. I hug him back for a second then step away, looking over what we've accumulated. A handwritten sheet of notes and a battered, second hand bible.

It's hardly a lot for the last line of defence but it's all we've got. I thought about some holy water, but Kev informed me only a priest can bless the water. Another thing that annoys me about the God theory. The God who is meant to love us all equally only allows a select few to do anything in His name.

I tell myself it's only an act. It's my sub-conscience that I'm really talking to, and I don't need props to do that.

I look through my notes. If I read these out, it will sound fake, even to me. I tear the paper up and let it fall to the floor.

'What are you doing?' asks Kev, his voice higher than it should be.

'I'm doing this my way,' I respond.

As I open my mouth to begin, the only thing that keeps going through my head is the title of a book I read years ago. Are You There God, It's Me Margaret. The absurdity of my situation hits me and instead of words, laughter comes out.

I laugh and laugh, bent double, clutching my stomach, tears streaming down my face. It feels good to let go and let all the emotions I've built up come out of me. Its somehow a better release than all the tears.

Kev isn't so sure. 'Are you ok?'

Hiccoughing a few times, I get control of myself. Wiping the tears from my face, I nod. 'Yes. Sorry, I don't know what happened there.' But I do know I am one step away from total hysteria, and I must get a grip if this is to have any chance.

Without a word to Kev, I walk into the kitchen, get a glass of water and take a long drink. I take a couple of deep breaths, and calm myself down. I go back into the sitting room, put the half drank glass of water down, and say 'Let's begin.'

'God,' I start. I stretch my arms out as if to receive an embrace. I don't know why I do this, it just felt right. I am going to have to trust my instincts here.

'Hear me now in my hour of need. I come to you open minded and open hearted. And I ask of you, help me rid myself of this demon that resides in me. Grant me the strength to cast him out. Grant me the courage to try. Grant me the acceptance to live with the consequences of casting him out, whatever they may be.'

I am very much aware that I am kind of chanting, and my voice has the edge of a TV medium running a séance.

I glance at Kev as I say the last part, and he nods encouragingly. I am still not sure if he stays because he loves me, or because he loves what Scurra is subtly making me. It's a risk I need to take.

'God, I accept your teachings, and feel your love. I open myself up to you, come to me and fill me with light to cast out the darkness. Fill me with love to cast out the hatred. Fill me with humility to cast out the longing for power.

'In the name of the Father, the Son and the Holy Ghost, I cast you out Scurra.'

I have managed to lose the phoney sounding voice, and my words and tone sounds more like my own again. As I re-find my voice, my words get louder, stronger, more forceful and I am yelling now. My arms are waving wildly. My head is thrown back and the tendons stand out on my neck. Beads of sweat form in my hairline, running down my face, stinging my eyes, but I barely notice.

'In the name of God, I command you to leave me and go back to the depths of Hell from where you crawled up.

'Let darkness consume you once more as I step into the light.

'God's power works through me and He commands you to leave.'

Suddenly, I feel him coming back up. Elation courses through me. It's working. He's leaving. I let my guard down, happy to know I will soon be free.

His voice bursts from my mouth, loud and amused. 'Nice show.'

'In the name of God I command you to leave me.' My voice is equally loud, strong and unwavering.

My mouth forms a sneer, then a laugh. 'You don't even believe in God. For those words to have any power, you must believe in them. Can you do that Kayleigh? I don't think you can.'

I mustn't let his words affect me, but they do. He is right. I don't believe in any of this, and I was fooling myself thinking it would work.

'In the name of God, I command you to leave me.' I say it again, but my voice is weak. There is no conviction there. It's a whisper, a plea, rather than a command.

'You still amuse me, so for now, I will allow you to keep playing your games. Be warned, there will come a time when I am no longer amused and then I will consume you.'

He continues inside my head. 'And I know you don't really want me to go. But that will be our little secret.'

'Get out,' I scream in my head, but the only effect it has is to make Scurra laugh slightly then go silent.

'Kayleigh?' Kev places his hand on my shoulder. He sounds afraid, and the fear makes me snap out of the trance like state I was in. He didn't hear the last part of the exchange and he probably thinks I've gone completely nuts.

I slowly bring my arms back down. 'It's no use Kev. They are just words when I don't really believe them.'

'So that's it, you're just going to give in?'

'No. No I'm not giving in, just changing tactics. I've got another idea. It might upset you, but I think it's the only way. I understand if you don't want to be a part of it.'

'I don't know what it is, but if you think it could work, I'm with you.'

'Good.'

I reach into my jeans pocket and pull out my mobile. Scrolling through the contents, I find the one I am looking for. Home. I press call and listen to the phone ringing.

'Hello.'

It's Shaun. 'Hey Shaun, how you doing?' I ask, fighting to keep my voice even.

'Alright,' he responds, but something tells me he's not alright. His voice sounds weird, strained almost. I don't have time to worry about that now. I will talk to him when this is over.

'Is mum about?'

'Yeah.'

I hear him calling to her. 'Mum, there's something on the phone pretending to be Kayleigh.'

I freeze. I must have heard wrong. Before I can fully process the thought, mum's voice comes down the phone.

'Hi honey.'

I don't speak for a second.

'Honey?'

'Mum, what did Shaun say to you then?'

'Oh ignore him. He's got some long running joke going on that you have a demon inside you or something. He plays too many video games; his imagination is running wild. I've tried talking to him but he insists it's true, so now I've taken to just ignoring it.'

'Put him on.' I don't know what I will say to him, but I need to hear this from him.

'Nonsense,' says mum. 'I am not having you encouraging this fantasy or acknowledging it in any way. Now what did you want?'

I really want to talk to Shaun, find out how he knows, but having a fight with my mum now isn't going to help me. Plus, I don't want to accidentally drag Shaun into this mess. I make a mental note to talk to him about it when this is all over though.

'You know how you keep telling me I should go see your psychic? Well I've decided I'd like to.'

'Oh great dear. I think it will really help you. I've been asking her if she has a message from Emma or Zach for you, but she insists she would need to see you face to face. What changed your mind?'

'I guess I just figured it would be nice to hear from them,' I lie. 'Do you think she could fit me in today?'

'I'll give her a call and ask her. She's usually pretty busy, but she does her best to make room for her regulars.'

Mum goes to see her four or five times a week, I'm pretty sure that's a regular she won't want to upset.

'I'll text you the details just as soon as I have them.'

'Thanks. Bye mum. Go easy on Shaun.'

'Bye.' She hangs up.

'So your plan is to go to a psychic and try to talk to Zach or Emma?'

'Nope,' I respond. 'My plan is to go to a psychic and talk to your mum. She's the only one who can tell me how to control this thing. I just figured by telling mum I'd finally given in about wanting to talk to Emma and Zach it would make it easier. You know, less questions.'

'You don't believe in God, but you believe in this bullshit?'

'I'm not sure what I believe anymore. But one thing I am certain of, is the psychic won't be able to trick me with this. There is no way she can know the truth of what's happening. I'm just going to tell her you miss your mum and want to speak to her. Either we will get something useful, or she will invent some comforting platitudes.'

'I don't know about this. It's not something I want to do. My mother should be allowed to rest in peace.'

'You think she's at peace knowing what's happening here?' My voice comes out with a little more venom than I had intended.

His face falls. 'No,' he says, his voice barely above a whisper.

'Look, I'm sorry, I didn't mean that how it came out,' I back track, mentally kicking myself.

'Whatever,' he shrugs, 'let's just leave my mum out of this.'

'I'm sorry Kev, really I am, I know this is hard for you, but I can't leave her out of this. She is my last hope.'

Rolling his eyes, he relents.

'Ok, ok, we'll try it, but don't be surprised if it doesn't get us anywhere, and don't be upset if I walk out.'

Before I can answer, my phone vibrates in my hand.

'It's my mum. She's sent me the psychic's address. Her name is Sarah and she can see us at 6pm.'

I read him the address. 'Do you know where this is?'

'It's about an hour away.'

I check my watch. We have an hour and a half until 6pm. Just enough time to try and make myself look reasonably presentable again and get over there.

***

The drive over is fairly uneventful. We argue a little about the validity of psychics and whether or not there are genuine ones out there. Eventually, we agree that if their words provide a little comfort to someone in need, then maybe there's a place for them.

I want to point out that they are pretty much the same as having a religious belief but I stop myself. I don't want to fight with Kev, and I feel bad for keeping on knocking his beliefs. Even if they are stupid, he's not and I don't want him to ever think I feel he is.

The last part of the journey is mainly spent in silence, broken only by Kev's sat nav giving him instructions. I think back to when he said he might walk out. That's not so bad I reason. I can play on the he's so upset angle and maybe get something.

I don't know what I'm expecting Sarah's house to look like, but certainly not the neat detached house with perfectly manicured lawns and a swing set in the garden. As we pull up onto the drive, I ask 'Is this definitely the right place?'

'Yeah,' Kev grins. 'What were you expecting? A caravan.'

I laugh. 'Yeah, kind of.'

I take a deep breath and make sure Scurra is pushed as far down as I can get him. It wouldn't do to have him burst out of me in here. I don't know if psychics have any sort of moral code, but I'd bet my bottom dollar if that happened Sarah would be on the phone to my mum before I reached the car on the way out.

'Ready?' I ask Kev.

He nods and reaches up to press the doorbell. I hear the chimes echo through the house closely followed by light footsteps.

The door opens to reveal a woman in her mid-forties. She is wearing jeans and a Guns and Roses T-shirt.

My surprise must show on my face. 'Kayleigh?' She steps aside to make room. 'Come on in. If you wanted the head scarf and hoop ear-rings you should have called ahead.'

I look up sharply as I pass her. I see the amusement in her eyes and the slight smile, and I find myself smiling sheepishly back at her.

'Sorry,' I mumble.

'It's fine,' she laughs. 'Common misconception. I assume this is your first time visiting a psychic? Bit of a sceptic, but you're desperate enough to try anything now?'

She's good. Or maybe she just listens to my mum too much. Either way, there's something about her that I like.

As she talks, she leads us into a brightly lit lounge. It's very white, very modern and very normal. There are no incense sticks burning, no black cat and no crystal ball. I'm starting to feel rather stupid.

She gestures for us to sit and we do, side by side on a white leather couch. Sarah sits opposite us in a white leather recliner.

'This is my boyfriend, Kev,' I blurt out as I find my manners and finally introduce him.

'Hi.' She smiles in his direction then turns back to me. 'Your mum tells me that you want to make contact with some friends of yours who passed away. I don't think that's the case at all. It's something else isn't it.'

I nod. I can't seem to find my voice. Something about Sarah is calming, yet she makes me kind of nervous at the same time. It's a bizarre feeling and I don't like it. Briefly I wonder if she makes me calmer and Scurra more nervous. Her laugh cuts into my thoughts.

'Relax. I don't have to be psychic to know that. If that was it, you wouldn't look so scared and you would have been here weeks ago. Something bad enough to make a sceptic – sorry two sceptics – arrive at my door in such a hurry isn't so hard to spot. What's this really all about?'

I don't know what to say. Something about Sarah makes me want to tell her everything. As I try to organize my thoughts into something I can actually say out loud to a stranger without sounding deranged, Kev speaks for the first time.

'We want to talk to my mother. We have something going on that we think she might be able to help us with.'

'Ok,' nods Sarah. 'Try to relax, both of you, and picture your mother's face.' The last part is obviously meant for Kev but I try to do the same. It will give me something to focus on.

Sarah closes her eyes. I glance at Kev who shrugs and does the same.

As the silence descends on the room, I feel Scurra trying to push back up. 'No.' I tell him inside my head. 'Not here.'

'Oh, I think here is the perfect place. Let's show your little friend what real evil looks like.'

With an immense force of will, I push him back down. I feel myself becoming more drained. Keeping Scurra at bay is exhausting and I don't know how much longer I can do this.

Sarah's eyes fly open.

'There is an evil presence here. So evil I can't begin to go past it. I don't know what you two have been messing around with, and I don't want to know. Get out of my house.'

She speaks in an eerily calm voice. I can't seem to move. I am so tired my legs have turned to lead.

'Now!' she shouts.

Kev stands up and hauls me to my feet. Practically carrying me he drags me through the front door and down the driveway. Opening the passenger door, he helps me in. As he goes to shut the door, Sarah comes running towards the car.

'Wait. I'm sorry. I panicked. There is something going on here Kayleigh. Something I don't understand, and something I won't take on. You are a good person. I hope you can fight this thing. Don't give up.'

'Please don't tell my mum about this,' I blurt out.

'It is not my place to interfere in a family's business. She won't hear it from me. I want to pretend like this never happened.'

I have so many questions I don't know how to begin, but Sarah doesn't give me a chance.

'I wish you good luck, and I really wish I could help you, but my children live here and I won't risk subjecting them to any evil forces. Please don't come back here.'

With a final half smile, she turns and walks back up the driveway, closing the front door, and, I imagine, treble bolting it.

Kev shuts my door, walks around the car and gets in the driver's seat.

'Wow,' he breathes as he starts the ignition.

That's the last thing I remember before he is shaking me awake. 'Kayleigh, we're home. Wake up.'

I force my eyes open and blink a few times, rubbing a hand over my face. I get out of the car and we head for the house.

'What time is it?'

'Half past seven.'

'I'm going to have a shower and go to bed. I'm so tired. We'll talk about this in the morning and plan our next move. Assuming you're still with me on this?'

'Always.'

***

I wake up the next morning still feeling tired, but it's a different sort of tired. It's the sort of tired people feel when they've given up and accepted their fate. It's not a good feeling and I need to shake it off. I have not accepted this and I won't accept it.

I hear a laugh in my head. I roll my eyes. Not again.

'You dare to roll your eyes at me?'

'You know what? I'm done with you. I'm done with you being in my head, done with you trying to take over. You picked the wrong girl.'

As I finish the thought I give an almighty push and he is gone before he gets the chance to reply. I am getting better at this. I can keep him down, as long as I don't let my guard slip.

It's exhausting keeping my guard up all the time. I must think of a way to get rid of him permanently.

I vow that today is the day. Whatever it takes I will get rid of him once and for all today or die trying. I am done with this.

I want to wake up happy and care free like I used to before any of this started. Be able to go out somewhere with Kev that is just for fun. To actually laugh again in a way that feels neither forced nor like the onset of hysteria.

With a new found resolve, I stand up out of bed. I get dressed and go towards the house in search of Kev and some breakfast. Not necessarily in that order.

'Morning,' I say to Kev as I walk into the kitchen.

'You ok?' he asks.

'Yeah, I think I actually am,' I say opening the cupboard to get some cereal.

'Sit down,' he says coming over and taking the cereal.

He pours it into a bowl and adds milk as I take a seat at the table next to the coffee he has already poured me. I take a sip. It's good.

'Thanks,' I say as he puts the cereal in front of me.

I start to eat and Kev sits opposite me. 'Aren't you having any?'

He laughs. 'I did - at breakfast time.'

'Huh?'

'It's after 11.'

'Really? Wow.' I appreciate a good lie in as much as the next person but 11?

I finish my breakfast in silence, thinking. Kev seems to sense I need this time to gather my thoughts and he drinks his coffee and flicks through the morning paper.

As I finish the last mouthful, an idea hits me and a plan starts to form. As soon as it starts, I know how it will go, and most importantly, I know it will work.

I curse myself inwardly for not thinking of it sooner.

I stand up, pushing the chair back and going to pour myself another coffee.

'Kev, I know what I'm going to do.'

Chapter 14

'I don't understand,' said Kev. 'How can you just give in?'

He stands up from his chair and walks around the table to where I am sat. Crouching next to me, he takes my hand.

'Don't you see? It's not giving in. Scurra wants to give me my deepest desire. He doesn't want to hurt me, maybe we misjudged him.'

Kev shakes his head, his expression sad. 'You're talking nonsense K. Do you really think he's going to give you this wish or whatever it is and then just go away? He will take over you completely and use you to do whatever he wants.'

'I'm done,' I respond. 'This is the way it's going to be.'

I have made my mind up. I don't think I can make Kev understand, but that's ok. I don't need him to understand. I know what I'm doing.

'He's got control of you. You have to fight him.'

'I don't want to fight him anymore.' I am shouting now. Kev is always the voice of reason and it's driving me nuts. I can think for myself. 'He's not in you, you don't get a say in this.'

'I thought we were in this together.'

'Well you thought wrong. You don't get a say in this when it's not living in you.'

Kev's shoulders slump. He leaves go of my hand and stands back up.

'Whatever.'

I know I've hurt him, and I hate myself for it, but it's the only way. I can't explain to him now. I have to let Scurra think he's won, and the only way to do that is to think and act like he has. If I slip for even a second, he will know.

'Please try to understand,' I say quietly.

'I do understand. You're tired, you've had enough and that thing has got it's claws into you. It's not too late to fight back.'

I laugh bitterly. 'Of course it's too late. It was always too late. I just didn't see it until now. It was clear right from the start. Those messages? You have the answers meant you had a way to understand what was going on through your mum. My message is so obvious now. I am his favourite. I was the one he was always going to end up after he had had his fun with you three. Do you see it now?'

'Honestly, no, but like you say it's not in me. Do what you have to do.'

He has given in far too easily. I'm worried he's going to try and interject.

'Kev, you have to let me do this. You have to trust me.'

'I do trust you, but this isn't you.'

'Yes, it is. I've made my mind up Kev. You know it's me, you just don't want to see it.'

'I don't know what to think anymore.'

'Think this – I love you and I always will, but this is bigger than me and you. It's bigger than love and I don't want to fight it anymore. I want to embrace it and just forget about it.'

'If you embrace it, you aren't forgetting it. You are letting it forget you.'

'It's the only way and you know it. I can't fight it for the rest of my life. Look what it did to your mum.'

It's a low blow, but it seems to work.

'You're right. I can't ask you to fight it, I won't be the one to make you live the life my mum did. I won't forget you K. I'll stay out of the way until you pack your things up and leave'

He walks over to me and kisses me lightly on the top of the head, stroking my hair with one hand. Without another word, he turns and walks out of the room.

Part of me wants to shout him back and ask him why he has given up on me so easily. I was scared he would try to talk me out of this, because I know if he tried hard enough he would succeed. He barely tried. Is Scurra right? Does he want rid of me and this is an easy way out for him?

I can't think of that now. I have to end this thing with Scurra once and for all. I slowly relax my mind, letting Scurra float up to the surface. He's mad.

His voice bursts from my mouth, stronger and more powerful than I've ever heard it. His presence overwhelming me more than ever before.

'You will not push me down again. I am done playing games.'

'Me too,' I respond meekly. My voice sounds weak even to me. What's the point in trying to sound strong anymore? I am not fighting him; I might as well go easy. 'You win. Grant me my darkest desire.'

'And in return?'

'You know.'

'I want to hear you say it.' He's playing with me.

'I thought we were done playing games.' Ok, I won't go that easily, I still have a little bit of pride.

'As you wish. Tell me your deepest desire'

A wash of shame floods me. I feel my face burning red. 'I can't say it out loud.' My voice is barely a whisper.

'A shameful desire. Oh, they are the best ones. You should be loud and proud.'

I have to play this bit just right, lure him in. Let him think what comes next was his idea. 'I'm sorry, I thought I could do this but I can't.'

'What?' he roars.

I'm terrified now, so the next thing I say is no act. 'I daren't tell you.'

He goes quiet for a second. I know I haven't lost him. I can still feel him at the front of mind, the sensation like a giant cockroach running through my thoughts.

'Then show me.'

'How?'

'Imagine your deepest desire. Think of it exactly as you've always pictured it.'

'O…Ok,' I stutter.

I pause for a second. I can't let him think it's coming to me easily or he might be suspicious. I am relying on his joy at winning to dullen his senses.

Slowly, piece by piece I allow an image to form in my mind.

A large chest comes into view. It is like an old fashioned pirate's chest only it's as black as the blackest night. A large silver padlock appears holding the chest closed.

'You want a treasure chest?'

'No, I want what's inside it.'

'It must be extremely depraved if you can't even allow yourself to see it.' The glee in his voice, my voice, is evident.

Easy now, don't go too far. 'I have spent a long time trying not to think of this, I have hidden it away, even from own subconscious.'

It's a lie, but as I had hoped, Scurra is too caught up in the thought of taking me completely to notice.

'I am going to enjoy this very much,' he says. He is back to talking in my head, his voice smug.

I see a shadow fall over the chest. I haven't added a shadow to the mental image. It is him.

'Open it,' he commands.

I visualise a key appearing in the padlock and turning. The padlock opens and the lid slowly begins to raise.

I don't want to seem too eager, so I let it close again before it opens more than an inch.

'Sorry,' I say. 'Let me try again.'

'Let me make it easy for you, now we are going to be a team. The more depraved it is, the better. I am not here to judge you, I am here to make your wish come true, whatever it is.'

That's my cue. I allow the lid of the chest to open all the way. As the black shadow that is Scurra leans over to look, I visualise a foot, my foot, pushing him inside the chest. I catch him off balance and he falls in head first. The lid slams shut, and the padlock locks.

I can hear Scurra cursing me with all the Demons of Hell, banging on the inside of the chest. For good measure, I visualise three thick metal chains wrapping themselves around the chest and locking.

Satisfied with the prison I have created, I push it down to the very bottom of my sub conscious. It's easy this time. I'm not fighting anyone anymore. I am very much back in control of my mind. The chest is something that will float around with the other things from the past I would rather forget. My psych professor would have a field day with this.

I didn't realise I had stood up from the chair until my knees buckled and I tumbled to the floor. I am laughing deliriously as I land. I have done it. I am free.

'Kev,' I shout, still laughing.

He comes in cautiously. I use every little bit of will power to get control of myself. If I want to get him to believe it's me, I can't be hysterical.

'It's over,' I say more calm than I feel. I feel in control for the first time since Zach died. It's a good feeling being boring old me again.

'Really?' Kev asks, frowning, sceptical.

'Really,' I reply, getting up from the floor and going to him. 'Look at me, and you'll know.'

Holding me by my shoulders he looks deep into my eyes. It's like he's looking into my very soul.

'It's really you. The yellow's gone.'

I nod agreement. I could never see the yellow in my own eyes, but I know the colour he's talking about. It's the flash of yellow I saw in his eyes when Scurra was in him.

'It's really me. We did it.'

'You did it,' he says, pulling me to him. We hold each other for a long time. He squeezes me so hard my ribs hurt but I don't care. I don't want him to ever let go. We stand holding each other for what feels like a lifetime. Laughing, crying, enjoying each other, enjoying being free.

Finally, he releases me. Taking my hand, he leads me to the sitting room. We sit side by side on the couch. Kev keeps looking at me like he can't quite believe I am here.

'What changed your mind? What made you fight? How did you beat him?' He has a lot of questions but I can understand that. I would have too if this was the other way around. As I ponder how to begin, he smiles.

'Sorry, that's a lot of questions at once.' He knows me so well.

I laugh a little. 'It is a lot of questions, I'm going to answer them all, but first I'm going to do this.'

I lean over and kiss him hard on the mouth. He meets my kiss with his own. It tastes of longing, desperation, and something more primal that I can't place. It tastes right. I don't want to stop, I want to make love to him right then and there. The desire I feel for him feels normal, clean, untainted. It is borne of love. I know I have to answer his questions first though, put this whole thing behind us once and for all.

I pull away and begin my story.

'As I ate breakfast this morning, I was thinking of my next move. I was intent on getting a hold of that Ouija board like we discussed months ago. It was the only other thing I could think of. I don't know who I was hoping to speak to or how they could help, but it seemed like a start point. I knew it had to be that exact one. I don't know how but I did.

'I was trying to work out how I would get it, and a stupid thought crossed my mind. If Scurra wanted to grant my deepest desire, I should ask him to get me that board.

'And that's when it hit me. My deepest desire wasn't to get a Ouija board, that was just a tool to achieve my desire. The desire was to get rid of Scurra.

'I devised a plan that would lead to him trapping himself inside a locked box in my head. I told him my greatest desire was inside that box. And it was. The desire to have him be locked in the box.

'He was so convinced he had broken me that I was able to trick him.'

'That's genius,' Kev said when I had finished. 'His own self confidence was his down fall. It didn't even occur to him that you wouldn't give up. But why couldn't you tell me that beforehand? Don't you trust me?'

'Of course I trust you, but I had no way of telling you without letting him know something was going on. You had to react that way for him to believe it was real. I'm sorry.'

'It's ok, I get it. I'm sorry too.'

I look at him, puzzled. He answers my unasked question.

'For walking away so easily. I'd like to say it was because I knew you had a plan, but the truth it I was scared and when you said you had given in, it was easier to give in too and just walk away.'

'None of that matters now. Let's just put all of this behind us and start over.'

'Let's get married.'

'Is that a proposal?'

'Well not exactly, I intend to do it right.'

I smile. We will be together forever. I know we will. I picture our wedding. All of our friends and family there, me dressed in white, him looking sexy in a black tux. The church all decorated in purple and silver.

I realise he's just said something.

'What?' I ask, pulled back to reality.

'I said is it really over?'

'It's over,' I tell him. And I really believe it is.

Standing in front of the full length mirror, Kev adjusts his cuff links for the one hundredth time. Satisfied, he reaches for his suit jacket and puts it on. He smooths down the lapels and removes a bit of imaginary lint from his shoulder.

There's a knock on his room door and he turns toward it. 'It's open,' he calls.

He wonders who it will be this time. He's already had two maids come in to see if he needs anything. He's glad they chose this hotel for the wedding, even if it was more than they could really afford. The service was second to none and it really was beautiful.

His best man has already been in and done the obligatory speech about how Kayleigh is the right one for him and how good they are together. He didn't need it. Nothing could tear him away from this wedding.

He feels a little sad that Zach isn't his best man, but he pushes the thought away. Nothing is going to ruin today.

'Dad,' Kev says, his face breaking into a grin. 'What are you doing here? You should be downstairs.'

'Just wanted to have a quick chat.' He hands a Kev a small glass of whiskey, and clinks his own against it. 'Cheers.'

They drink and Daniel sits on the bed, his expression grave.

'Son, I just wanted to say it's not too late to change your mind. You don't have to go through with this if you don't' want to.'

'What? I thought you liked Kayleigh.'

'I do like her. I like her a lot, but I know you've had second thoughts a few times. It's like she has some sort of a hold over you.'

Kev goes to interrupt him, but holding up a hand to silence him, he continues. 'When she's not around, you seem so adamant you want to end things, then as soon as she comes into the room, it's like she's the centre of your world. Does she have something over you.'

Sitting down himself, Kev says 'No. It's not like that. It's just talk. You know how it is, sometimes you think about how your life could be different, but I love Kayleigh and I'm marrying her dad.'

Kev's dad claps him on the back. 'Ok son, I shouldn't have said anything, I just wanted to make sure you wanted to do this.'

Standing, Kev says 'I'm sure. Let's go.'

***

Kev stands at the altar, nervously checking his watch. 'She's late,' he says to no one in particular.

Before anyone can reassure him, the organ starts to play and there she is. His beautiful bride.

Kayleigh walks down the aisle toward him, linking Peter. Peter's face beams proudly.

Kayleigh is a vision of beauty. Her dress is so white it almost hurts Kev's eyes to look at her. Her hair curls just right beneath her veil, and she is carrying a beautiful bouquet of purple flowers interlaced with white.

His eyes scan the crowd, all their friends and family. He sees Kathy, her eyes filled with tears already.

Kathy catches him looking at her. She smiles as Kayleigh reaches him and he smiles back.

He turns his attention back to Kayleigh, the love of his life, his bride-to-be. This is going to be the happiest day of their lives.

'Dearly beloved,' Father Spencer begins. 'We are gathered here today…'

He stops and looks at Kev and Kayleigh uncertainly.

'Is something wrong?' asks Kayleigh.

'No. No, I'm sorry, I just… Nothing.'

Looking embarrassed, Father Spencer continues. Kayleigh looks at Kev and raises an eyebrow.

Kev shrugs slightly.

Father Spencer knows what she is, what she has trapped inside of her. Maybe he even knows that sometimes, she lets a little bit of it out. He doesn't know the full extent of it of course, but he knows something is a little off with her. Priests always have this reaction to her. She has grown used to it. It's a small price to pay to marry the man she loves.

Father Spencer continues with the vows. Kayleigh and Kev repeat them back to him, saying I do in all the right places, but neither of them are really paying attention to him. They each have their own internal battles going on.

The thought going through Kev's mind is. 'I can't do this; I don't love her anymore. I don't want to be with her. I should leave before it's too late. She can't stop me, not again, not in front of all these people. My dad won't mind; I think he'll secretly be pleased'

The sweat stands out on his brow. One of the guests nudges her partner. 'He's having second thoughts that one.'

'He's just nervous.'

Kayleigh sees the look come over Kev, a flicker of uncertainty. She can't allow him to leave her, she loves him too much.

She knows what to do. It's not like she hasn't done it before. She thinks of a chest. A black chest. It opens ever so slightly, and a thin tendril of black comes out.

She slams it shut before any more can escape.

Kev looks at Kayleigh, his face puzzled. He could swear he just saw a flash of yellow in her eyes. It's gone as quickly as it came and Kev tells himself he's being stupid. All of that's behind them now.

He smiles at Kayleigh. He is marrying the love of his life and he couldn't be happier.

'You may kiss the bride,' finishes Father Spencer.

Pushing back her veil, Kev does just that. As she kisses him back, she smiles and thinks to herself, 'Sometimes, a girl has more than one desire.'

16310683R00065

Printed in Great Britain
by Amazon